Don Quixote

Edited by Jane Chisholm
Designed by Brian Voakes
Cover design by Glen Bird
Cover photography: Rider & horse © Lee Snider/
Photo Images/CORBIS
Windmills © Nik Wheeler/CORBIS
Series designer: Mary Cartwright

Don Quixote

From the story by
Miguel de Cervantes Saavedra
retold by Henry Brook

Illustrated by Ian McNee

Contents

About Don Quixote

The story by Miguel de Cervantes, of a middle-aged landowner in rural Spain who dreams of becoming a knight, is one of the foundation stones of world literature. For some novelists, it is the blueprint for all works of imaginative writing. Within its vast bulk - the original two parts are well over 400,000 words long - Cervantes explores all the major themes that preoccupy authors and their readers. Conceived as a parody of the chivalric tales that were popular in Europe at the time, he switches between genres as he pleases, touching on comedy, drama, tragedy and adventure. As the tale unfolds, we are introduced to stories within stories, dream sequences, bits of poetry and scenes of hard-hitting realism. It is full of surprises - perhaps the greatest being that, although every page still seems fresh and relevant today, it was written almost 400 years ago, at the very beginning of the 17th century.

The novel opens with the simple description of a man who reads so many stories about knights and their fantastic adventures, he loses all grip on reality and decides to set out on a chivalric quest of his own. Dressed in a makeshift knight's costume of rusty iron and cardboard, Don Quixote, as he calls himself, roams the parched landscape of southern Spain, looking for damsels to rescue and ogres to slay. In his deluded state of mind, he sees the world in a different way from the rest of us. A line of windmills is really a gang of menacing giants. A flock of sheep is a marauding army of enemy knights. Like an artist or writer, the aspiring knight fills his world with incredible encounters, amazing sword fights and bizarre coincidences. In this way, he turns dull, everyday events into magical adventures.

Don Quixote has become quite deranged, but Cervantes' first stroke of genius is to give his hero the very knightly qualities he aspires to. The man is polite, gracious and wise. We might chuckle at his vision of the world, but we can't dismiss him as a fool. Much of what he says is profound and insightful, and his fevered imagination looks rich and exciting compared with real life. The author's second masterstroke comes when he has Don Quixote recruit a tubby, local farmer to act as his squire. After only a few chapters of the novel, we are introduced to Sancho Panza.

At first, Sancho seems little more than a village idiot riding on a donkey behind his superior. But his rough country wit, lively tongue and insatiable appetite for the good things in life - dishes piled high with of pigs' trotters, for example - quickly establish him as one of the greatest comedy double act partners in literature. The knight and squire seem made for each other. As Sancho's bawdy nature emerges, Don Quixote's courtly manners and highbrow outlook on life are brought to the surface. The conversations between the two friends are pure slapstick, with each of them struggling to assert their contrasting philosophy on life. But it is during these moments in the book when Don Quixote seems most kingly and noble.

In a recent survey of one hundred of the world's greatest novels, *Don Quixote* stood out as the book many people admired above all others. In his simple story of the two wandering companions, Cervantes somehow managed to explore what it means to be alive and to dream of a better life . He takes us into a world full of masks and shadows, where nothing is as it appears at first glance. The knight's tale forces us to question how we see ourselves, how we decide what is real and what is make-believe. This is the underlying aim of all great books, to urge us to think again about how we look at the world around us. *Don Quixote* is first and foremost a work of entertainment, and Cervantes wanted his readers to have a good laugh at the knight's antics. But the book also carries a powerful message: if we want something badly enough, and we dare to dream of having it, then we just might succeed.

Part One

The First Sally

Concerning our valiant hero, the renowned Don Quixote de la Mancha, and how he became a knight

In a small village in the dry and dusty La Mancha region of Spain, the name of which I can't quite remember, there lived a country gentleman who loved to read chivalric adventure stories. By this I mean those incredible tales of knights and damsels, wizards and dragons, enchanted forests and magic swords stuck fast in boulders. They include the legends of King Arthur and his Round Table, Merlin and Lancelot and all that courtly gobbledygook. Our gentleman couldn't get enough of these fantastic yarns, and spent his every spare minute - and every last penny - collecting a great library of them.

Not that he was a wealthy man who could afford to lie around reading books all day. No, he was only a plain hidalgo, which is someone richer than a peasant but poorer than a nobleman. His surname was something like Quixada, or Quixano - which means *jawbone* or *thighbone* to someone with a grasp of the Spanish language - but here the facts become murky. What I am sure of though, is that his house was modest, his horse mangy and his meals minimal. He owned a few acres of farmland and lived off the rental income they provided, supporting his own needs, a housekeeper the wrong side of forty and a niece the right side of twenty. Our bookworm hidalgo was almost fifty years old, and his flesh was dried-up and withered after spending so many summers under the brutal La Mancha sun. But, he was still fit and healthy, an early riser and a keen huntsman. Or at least he was, until he discovered those stories I mentioned.

The problem was that each tale he finished, describing the adventures of valiant knights in far-off kingdoms, only left him hungry for another. Soon, he was reading day and night, and his eyes were bloodshot and crazed. He locked himself away in his library, lost in a fantastic realm of witches, elves, haunted castles and heroic quests. On the odd occasions he did venture out, he would get into arguments with his best friends - the local priest and the village barber - about who was the strongest knight or which chivalric adventure was the most impressive.

His friends thought he was joking, of course, but the truth was that our hidalgo had become so bedazzled by his books, he was starting to think the stories were all true. Finally, he went completely crazy. Waking up in his reading chair one morning, he declared: "Right, I've made up my mind. I'm going to be a knight errant."

"A what?" cried his niece, who had been

eavesdropping in the hallway, a little concerned about the strange hours her uncle was keeping.

"Are you really so ignorant, dear child?" he asked seriously. "A knight errant is a wandering doer of good deeds, a righter of wrongs, friend to the unfortunate, rescuer of fair maidens and a slayer of fearsome dragons."

"But, uncle," she gasped, "there are no dragons in Spain. And who are these fair maidens that need rescuing?"

Ignoring her protests, the hidalgo rushed to the attic of his house. After rummaging around in some boxes for most of the morning, he found an ancient, rusting (and rather smelly, I might add) suit of arms that had belonged to one of his forefathers. He scrubbed and polished this metal suit as though his life depended on it, but it still looked like a pile of old pots and saucepans. Even so, he was very proud of it. Then he noticed that the hinged visor from the helmet was missing. Undaunted, he constructed one from some cardboard his housekeeper had left lying around. After hours of huffing and puffing – and lots of creaking – he was dressed in his iron suit and felt ready for anything.

"And now, to my faithful steed," he announced in a bold voice.

Our hidalgo's nag was as worn out and wrinkled as its rider. Her rib bones stuck out like cats twisting around in a sack. She hadn't made it up to a full gallop for donkeys' years. But, in the eyes of the deluded hidalgo, she was a valiant warhorse, faster than the wind, and stronger than that brawny Greek hero, Hercules.

"I name you Rocinante, Queen of the hacks," he told her. "And now, I must have a suitable name for myself."

After almost a week of frantic muttering, pacing around his library and tugging on his wispy beard, our hidalgo decided on the title *Don Quixote* - that is *Sir Thighpiece*. Only noblemen were allowed to call themselves *Don*, but he was too demented to care. To top it off, he gave himself the title *de La Mancha* - so that anyone who witnessed his great deeds would know where he came from, I suppose.

"All that remains," he announced, "is for me to dedicate my life to my lady."

"But, do you have a lady?" sobbed his poor niece, who was still trying to make him see reason after enduring a week of his ravings. "I don't think that you do."

"Nonsense," he barked. "All knights have a lady. When I vanquish a giant, or topple a tyrant, I will parade him before her, as a tribute to my love and my loyalty."

"But uncle, you don't know any ladies," she cried, wondering if this argument might at last bring him to his senses.

Racking his brains, Don Quixote remembered some gossip he'd heard about a young peasant girl who lived in the nearby village of El Toboso. She was supposed to be a real heartbreaker, prettier than a polished gold coin, fresher than a field of daisies.

Losing all grip on reality, he decided she must be a lonely princess and he fell desperately in love with her, instantly, even though he'd never cast eyes on her. He informed his niece of this new development.

"What's her name?" she demanded, trying to trick him. "I think you've made the whole thing up."

"The finest ladies in the true histories of knights are often called *Dulcinea*," he replied. "So, my lady must be the *Dulcinea del Toboso* - and to her I dedicate my life. Now, don't try to stop me. Into the fray I must go."

He fixed his sword in its shoulder scabbard, took a cracked, old lance and leather shield from a rack on the wall, and marched off to the stable. A few minutes later, he was riding out onto the plain that surrounded the village, eager and ready for his first knightly challenge.

But Don Quixote hadn't gone far when he was struck by a terrible thought: he was a knight who hadn't been knighted.

"What an oversight," he gasped, jerking bolt upright in his saddle. "I must find a lord or lady who has the power to knight me. I don't want people to call me a fraud. In the meantime, I will have to call myself an apprentice knight."

All day long he rode around the sun-baked plain, looking for his first adventure, but nothing happened worth mentioning. By dusk, he and his nag were weary and starving. As the light faded, Don Quixote saw an inn a few miles away and turned towards it.

"Perhaps we can find shelter at that distant castle?" he told Rocinante, and, clicking his spurs, he tried to tempt her into a canter.

The inn was one of those humble places for weary voyagers that used to be scattered all over the rutted highways of Spain. It was crumbling and weathered, and the innkeeper was a portly rogue who'd knocked around in some of the seediest parts of the kingdom. There was a low mud wall around the perimeter, a few shabby buildings for guests and animals to sleep in, and a bed of straw and dung spread all over the yard. Two dirty-faced peasant girls in torn dresses were sitting on a bench by the front door. They watched in amazement as a man dressed in rusty iron and a cardboard faceplate emerged out of the gloom.

"Good evening, fine ladies," he called to them. "I am the apprentice knight, Don Quixote de La Mancha. Please summon a trumpeter to announce my arrival."

To the eyes of this chivalric lunatic, the inn was a great castle with silver-spired towers. The peasant girls were nothing less than beautiful maidens who had been dispatched to greet him. So he was a little put out when they stared at each other and burst into fits of giggles.

"You must know it is only proper," blustered Don Quixote, "for an illustrious knight to receive his trumpet blast. Even an apprentice knight."

At that moment, a pig-handler stepped out of the inn and sounded his horn to round up his grunting animals for the night. Don Quixote heard this parp, and the noise of the pigs, and mistook the din for a chorus of pipes and trumpets. He rode up to the door at once and the two girls shied away in terror.

"Do not fear me, ladies," Don Quixote called down to them. "It is my sworn duty to protect all highborn maidens."

"What's all this talk about maidens?" roared the innkeeper, stepping into the yard. "If it's a bed you're wanting, mister, you're out of luck. We're full and I..." He was about to continue, but when he looked up at Don Quixote in his madcap iron suit, with the cracked lance and warped shield, the innkeeper was lost for words.

"Might you be the master of this castle?" Don Quixote asked politely.

"I suppose I might," replied the innkeeper, who fancied himself as a bit of a joker and had now guessed that the rider before him must be madder than a box of frogs.

"Can I take shelter then, dear sir," asked Don Quixote, "inside the walls of your sturdy keep?"

"I've already said there are no beds," the innkeeper answered gruffly. "Er, I mean, the royal apartments are all occupied."

"No matter," said Don Quixote. "A good knight is used to suffering and hardship. He should be happy to sleep on the rough ground, eat wild herbs and berries and use a rock for his pillow."

"Oh, you're a knight are you?" cried the rascally innkeeper.

"I am," Don Quixote said proudly. "Well, almost. I seek a kind lord who will dub me with his sword."

"I understand," answered the innkeeper. "We'll talk of this later. For now, I have a house full of guests to look after, but I'll send some food out to you when I get a chance."

"Most gracious of you," replied Don Quixote. Ten minutes later, Rocinante was safely stabled and the apprentice knight was chomping away at a dish of cold sardines and a hunk of black bread, almost as smelly as his suit of iron.

As soon as his hunger was satisfied, his longing to be knighted prompted him to send one of the peasant girls to fetch the innkeeper.

"Oh Lord," Don Quixote told the bemused man when he stumbled out of the inn, "I can wait no longer for the good deed you must do. When will you lead me to your castle's chapel, so that I may keep the vigil of arms and earn my knighthood?"

"*Wiggle* his *palms*?" said one of the peasant girls, baffled by his words.

"*Burn* his *kite-wood*?" said the other girl, equally puzzled.

"I have no chapel, good knight," replied the innkeeper, ignoring the girls. He knew that Don Quixote was talking about the ancient custom of a knight standing guard at some landmark, a chapel or bridge, for example. If necessary the knight would defend his post to the death, as a demonstration of his loyalty. I've already said this innkeeper thought of himself as a bit of a joker. Now he decided to have some fun at Don Quixote's expense. "But you can keep your vigil here, in the yard, under the stars. If you want me to knight you, guard my courtyard."

"With pleasure," replied Don Quixote.

The innkeeper was about to go in when he remembered something and spun on his heels. "Wait a moment," he barked. "Do you have any luggage with you, apprentice knight?"

"Only my weapons, my horse and my courage," answered the nutty knight.

"I thought so. Where do you keep your cash?"

"I had not considered such practical matters," answered Don Quixote. "In all the stories I've read of knights and their good deeds, money has never been mentioned. Brave hearts are given free board and lodging wherever they wander."

"Money talks and knights can walk," spat the innkeeper. "You need a squire who can look after your practical matters, while you go off chasing dragons or whatever it is you do. You can owe me for the meal, but don't ask for breakfast. Get on with your vigil."

With that he turned and stomped off to his kitchen. Don Quixote picked up his suit of iron and his weapons and walked into the middle of the courtyard, taking up position next to a water trough. While he circled this trough, arms at the ready, inside the tavern the innkeeper told his guests about the madman outside and his ambition to be a knight. Everyone laughed and took turns to peek through the window at the patrolling blockhead.

A few hours passed, then a muleteer who was resting at the inn went out to water his animals. Approaching the trough, he saw the flash of a lance in the dark.

"Stand back, rash knight," boomed Don Quixote, lurching out of the shadows. "I defend this magic well to the death, as my vigil of arms demands."

"But I must moisten my mules," cried the peasant. "And it's a trough, not a well. Get out of my way, you dolt." Without another word he pushed past the guardian of the water trough. Whereupon Don Quixote walloped him on the head with his lance and knocked him unconscious.

"My first good deed is done," cried Don Quixote, with great satisfaction. "When he recovers, I must send this vanquished foe to pay his respects to my lady, Dulcinea."

Moments later, another muleteer stepped out of the inn and approached the water trough. This time Don Quixote gave no warning. His lance flashed and the muleteer lay stunned in the straw and dung of the yard. "Help me, lads," he whimpered.

Hearing their friend's plea, the rest of the muleteers dashed out of the inn. Don Quixote charged at them with his trusty lance, which was looking pretty buckled by now.

"A swarm of villainous knights attacks me," Don Quixote cried. "But I will defeat them all, as a beekeeper swats aside bees."

The muleteers started lobbing stones at the crazed apprentice knight. It was the best Don Quixote could do to back away, defending himself behind his cracked leather shield. Hearing the sounds of a raging battle developing outside, the innkeeper ran out and called for calm.

"He's mad as a hatter, boys," he told the muleteers. "Even if he killed one of you, he'd walk out of court a free man. The police won't charge someone who's so clearly insane. Let me deal with him."

The innkeeper was miffed that his prank had backfired on him. It was about time he got rid of this screwball, he decided.

"Dear Knight," he said craftily, approaching Don Quixote, "forgive this rabble for their impudence and lay down your lance. You've proven yourself to be a courageous fighter, so I think we can proceed with the dubbing without delay."

Don Quixote was quite overcome with excitement, while the innkeeper sent one of his maids for the *Book of Knightings* – in truth simply a ledger of how many mules had passed through his stables and the revenue from the sale of their manure.

"I'm sure we don't need to bother with any chapel," said the innkeeper. "The field of battle is a noble enough place for a knighting. Kneel," he ordered. Don Quixote bowed down obediently in the straw and dung.

"I hereby appoint you to the order of righteous knights," the innkeeper cried, smacking Don

Quixote across the back with his own sword. "Mark it in the book," he told the peasant girl, who couldn't even write her own name. "Right then, Knight, off you go and do your duty."

Don Quixote jumped to his feet. "My Lord, I owe you everything."

"Yes, yes," snapped the innkeeper, anxious to be rid of this dangerous fruitcake. "You owe me for a fish supper, but we'll forget about that. Off you go on your good-deeding and wrong-righting."

"At once," shouted Don Quixote. He hurried to the stables and was riding out onto the plain, just as the first rosy fingers of dawn were stretching out across La Mancha.

He hadn't gone far when he spotted a group of

silk merchants and their assistants approaching along the road.

"Here is an opportunity for gallantry," Don Quixote explained excitedly to Rocinante. "These knights shall be made to pay tribute to my lady."

The brave knight rode up to the traders and blocked the road before them.

"Halt, varlets," he cried. "None shall pass, until they confess that in all the world there is no maiden more beauteous than the Empress of La Mancha, my Dulcinea del Toboso."

The traders and their servants stared at each other. They soon guessed that the strange figure before them must be a hooting madman.

"Let's have a look at her then," called one of the party, unable to resist taunting the lunatic. "We need to see her peerless beauty before we can confess to it."

"You're missing the point," explained Don Quixote impatiently. "You must confess before seeing her, or face me in knightly combat."

"That's silly," replied the comedian, to the titters of his friends. "Mind you," he continued, "I'm sure she's very pretty if she commands the heart of such an impressive knight as yourself. She couldn't be any old sloppy chops, could she?"

"*Sloppy chops?*" screamed Don Quixote in outrage. "Prepare to do battle, you impudent knave."

The fearless knight lifted his battle-worn lance and kicked Rocinante with his spurs, so hard she charged forward in a fast trot, if not exactly a gallop. It would have been a very bad thing for the trader if she hadn't stumbled and crashed to the ground. But she did and her master flew through the air and landed with a loud thud in a ditch at the side of the road.

"Cowards," cried Don Quixote, from inside his bent iron suit. "You'd all be mincemeat if my horse hadn't fallen."

One of the footmen accompanying the merchants took umbrage at this insult. He picked up Don Quixote's battered lance and broke it over the knight's cardboard visor. The lance broke into splinters and the footman picked up the largest piece and used it to thrash the prostrate knight until he was black and blue – even with the protection of his iron suit. Don Quixote was left stranded at the roadside, too sore, bruised, beaten and exhausted even to attempt standing.

Hours later, a farmer from the same village as our mad hidalgo passed by on a donkey. He heard a whimper from the side of the road. Dismounting, he inspected the heap of iron and cardboard stranded in the dust. It was only when he wiped the muck away from the hidalgo's face with his handkerchief that he recognized the face of Señor Quixano.

"What are you doing down in this ditch, my friend?" the farmer asked.

"I am a famous knight and courtly hero and am pursuing my mission to do good deeds," answered Don Quixote.

"Of course you are," said the farmer. "And here I

was thinking you were that old boy who lives in my village, stranded in a hole."

"I have been battling legions of enemies," Don Quixote continued. "Will you let me rest in your castle for the night, kind lord?"

Scratching his head, the farmer loaded Don Quixote onto his donkey and set off for the village. Every step of the way, the knight was rambling on about giants and trolls and the magnificent beauty of his lady.

"I get more sense out of my donkey," the farmer whispered to himself. By nightfall, they were back home and Don Quixote was tucked up in his old bed, sleeping soundly.

Giant Killer

How Don Quixote engaged a squire and set off on his adventures, the first being that famous battle with the giants of the air

The bruised and battered hidalgo had been sorely missed by his friends the priest and the barber, as well as by his niece and housekeeper. They all fussed around his bedside, trying to convince him that he was just a simple man and that all this talk of knights and doing good and glorious deeds was ridiculous.

"But this world of ours needs a new age of chivalry," Don Quixote argued. "I will chase all the giants, evil knights and enchanters out of the kingdom and make it a better place."

"You need some rest, my friend," replied the priest. "Let some other hidalgo worry about the giants and enchanters."

While nobody was looking, the housekeeper carted her master's books out to the courtyard and burned them to ashes.

"Evil things," she cried, staring into the flames of the bonfire she'd made. "The poor man would still have his wits about him if he hadn't opened your wretched pages."

For two weeks, Don Quixote rested in his house, giving his carers the impression that he was slowly regaining his sanity. At times the hidalgo spoke a lot of sense, about good conduct, decency and the responsibilities of the king's subjects. But every so often, after delivering a speech that had impressed everyone with his wisdom, he would come out with one of his tall tales about damsels and dragons. Shaking their heads, his friends would tell each other he would soon recover from this *brain fever*. What they didn't know was that Don Quixote had sold a parcel of his land to finance his next quest, and was trying to find himself a squire, as the innkeeper had recommended.

The only man who showed any interest in the job was a fat little farmer named Sancho Panza, who was known around the village as a bit of a dunce. Any man with a brain to rattle in his head would have realized that Don Quixote had bats in the belfry, and even Sancho Panza had his doubts.

"It sounds like hard work, being a squire," Sancho told his prospective employer. "Basically, I have to wander around the wilder parts of the country, in charge of your wallet and your closet. We'll be slaying dragons and rescuing maidens and generally getting into hot water, when I could be at home with my family, diving into a nice plate of pigs' trotters."

Sancho Panza liked his food. And his wine. And his afternoon naps.

"But squires," replied Don Quixote patiently, "always end up receiving great prizes of land and gold from the grateful knights they serve."

"Do they really?" squealed Sancho Panza with delight, his eyes lighting up.

"Of course they do. Each time I vanquish a giant or defeat a rival knight in a joust, I automatically inherit his wealth and kingdom. When the time comes, I will not forget my loyal attendant. You will no doubt end up as the governor of some rich island or fertile province."

"That's more like it," cried Sancho Panza, licking his lips. "My own island, you say? I'll pack my bags and saddle my donkey."

"Squires walk behind their masters," said Don

Quixote, icily.

"This one doesn't."

"But they do in the stories."

"I haven't read the stories, so that doesn't matter."

"Perhaps in your case," said Don Quixote, nodding his head wearily, "we could make an exception."

They left in the dead of that night, without telling a soul.

By dawn, the two adventurers were out in the middle of a wide plain. La Mancha has lots of these plains. Shielding his eyes from the brilliant glare of the emerging sun, Don Quixote noticed thirty or forty windmills standing in the fields ahead of him.

Their long, wooden sails creaked and turned slowly on the breeze.

"Sancho," he called, "fortune is smiling on us."

"Is it?" answered the squire. "Does that mean it's time for breakfast?"

"This is no time for eating, you glutton. Look at those giants over there. I intend to engage them in battle, slay every one of them, and do Spain a great service. Men will write books about this battle, in centuries yet to come."

"What giants are you talking about?" asked Sancho.

"Over there," replied his master. "The ones with the thick bodies and the arms almost six miles long."

"Are you seeing things, Don Quixote?" Sancho cried. "Those are windmills. The arms are sails and they turn the millstones to crush the wheat. Those are our bread makers."

"Don't contradict me, squire. I know an army of fierce giants when I see one. If you do not wish to join me in the fray, you are excused. Wait here on your donkey."

Leaving his squire open-mouthed and amazed, Don Quixote spurred Rocinante into a canter – almost – and charged at the windmills.

"Get ready to fight, you rogues," cried Don Quixote. "Although I am only one knight, I have the bravery to match a thousand."

He gritted his teeth and made straight for the nearest tower. But, as he thrust the shaft of his lance into its sweeping sail, his weapon shattered and the huge arm plucked the knight off his horse and launched him through the air. He landed with a great boom, fifty yards distant, sending up a huge cloud of white dust.

"I told you they were windmills," said Sancho smugly, when he had trotted over on his donkey.

"You are a fool, squire," said a firm voice from inside the heap of iron, leather and cardboard on the ground. "Being a knight is no simple business. I have many enemies. When I charged at those giants, an evil enchanter..."

"Decanter? What's that when it's at home?" asked Sancho, his eyes lighting up with curiosity.

"A wizard, you ignoramus. Help me stand."

Sancho dropped down from his donkey, while Don Quixote continued his lecture on wizardry.

"This enchanter, flying by on an invisible horse or magic carpet, noticed my courageous charge and decided to rob me of the glory of victory. Immediately, he then transformed the giants into common windmills."

"I see," said Sancho, believing every word and helping his master to his feet. "A magic carpet did you say?"

"That is how enchanters get about."

"Sounds comfortable. Can you take a snooze on a flying carpet, or is the ride too bumpy?"

"But do not fear, Sancho," said Don Quixote, ignoring the question. "I shall vanquish this enchanter before he can do any more damage. Bring me my horse."

They rode about for a few more hours, then took shelter in a forest of green oaks. It was morning before they set out again, onto the wide plain.

A day's riding found them struggling over a high pass on a mountain road. Two friars in brown robes were coming towards them, accompanied by their servants. They were followed by a coach drawn by a team of white horses.

"Look Sancho," cried Don Quixote. "Those two fiends in cloaks must be the enchanter, who tricked me with the windmills yesterday, and his crafty assistant. They have kidnapped a princess riding in her carriage."

"Are you sure, sir," replied the squire. "Those look like friars to me, and seeing as this is the main road to Madrid, I reckon that coach is full of ordinary passengers."

"You are so easily taken in by his spells, Sancho," scoffed the knight. "This world is full of masks and shadows, and nothing is as it appears at first glance."

Without another word, Don Quixote urged Rocinante forward and raised his lance to the faces of the surprised monks.

"Hold, you diabolical enchanters," he roared. "Release the captive princess at once, or face my terrible wrath."

The two friars explained who they were and denied any knowledge of any princess or anything else that might possibly cause them to be delayed on their journey.

"You lying knaves," cried Don Quixote, charging at them. The men were so frightened they tumbled from their mounts. One of them fell and lay stunned on the road, while the other broke into an undignified sprint across the hillside. Don Quixote rode on to investigate the coach, while Sancho hurried over to the fallen friar and started tugging at his robes.

"I'll be having those," he cried. "My master's bested you, so they're the spoils of war. Squires are entitled to their fair share."

The friars' servants were clearly unfamiliar with this knightly tradition. They rushed over to their stricken master and thrashed Sancho Panza within an inch of his life. Up ahead, Don Quixote was addressing the puzzled occupant of the coach, an elderly woman on her way to visit her husband in Madrid.

"I am the renowned knight, Don Quixote de La Mancha," he announced. "I have liberated you from those ravishing enchanters, dear lady. All I ask in return, is that you turn your coach around and visit the village of El Toboso, where you must prostrate yourself before my mistress, Dulcinea, and testify to my bravery in her service."

"Out of the way, dimwit," cried one of the lady's porters, riding up on his mule and knocking Don Quixote's crooked lance to the ground. "We can't be delayed because of your tomfoolery. Be off with you."

"Dimwit, you dare to say?" roared Don Quixote. "Defend yourself, you varlet."

He drew his sword and curled it through the air. If the porter hadn't snatched a leather cushion from the roof of the coach and used it as a shield for his head, Don Quixote's blow would have cut him clean in two. Nimble as a cat, the porter twisted in his saddle, snatched his own sword from its scabbard and swung it towards the knight. The blade sliced through our hidalgo's flimsy helmet, chopping off one side of it – along with half of Don Quixote's ear. This wound so incensed the courageous knight, he stood up in his stirrups and brought his sword down with both hands on the porter's plump cushion shield. It was as though a mountain had landed on the poor man. Blood spurted from his ears and nostrils and his whole body quivered under the impact. He slid from his mule and collapsed at the side of the coach.

"Spare him any more violence, dear knight," called the lady from the window of her coach. "You have proved your bravery."

"Indeed I have," replied Don Quixote, fingering the gory stump of his ear. "Will you testify to it in front of my mistress, Dulcinea?"

"I will," promised the lady, who had decided it was best to play along with the madman and get moving with all possible haste.

"Come, Sancho," called the knight. "We must retire to some shady spot and treat my wounds."

The squire, his clothes torn and his face bloody from the beating he'd received, limped over to pick up his master's lance.

"Has the lady given you an island or a fertile province, for your weary squire to govern?" he asked with pleading eyes.

"Not this time, Sancho."

"That's a pity," the squire whimpered, climbing aboard his donkey. An hour later they were resting under a chestnut tree, bandaging Don Quixote's head, both of them groaning from their wounds. Sancho lit a fire and rummaged around in his saddlebags for some supplies.

"We have salami, a block of cheese, an onion and a loaf of bread," he declared. "A feast."

"Knights should be happy to eat nuts and berries for their dinner," replied Don Quixote. "They shy away from luxuries when they're on a quest."

"Fine," answered Sancho, stuffing his mouth with a handful of raw onion, "you do the shying and I'll do the feasting."

Don Quixote sighed and stared out at the fading light of dusk. That night he hardly slept a wink, his mind racing with thoughts of his lady and the dangerous adventures that awaited him. Sancho, on the other hand, fell asleep as soon as he'd finished eating and snored very heavily until morning.

At first light they broke camp, with Sancho complaining that squires needed their breakfast even if their masters didn't. They'd been following the road for an hour when Don Quixote saw a great cloud of dust, like a bank of fog, rushing towards them.

"This is it, Sancho," he cried. "At last I can prove myself a worthy knight. An army of bloodthirsty warriors is marching upon us."

"Or is it two armies?" replied Sancho calmly. "There's another dust cloud coming up behind us."

"Well spotted," said the knight, turning in his saddle. "There will be a great battle here today, between these rival armies. And Don Quixote will be in the thick of it."

"But who is it, doing all this fighting?" asked Sancho.

Don Quixote quickly outlined the structure of

both armies to his squire, the names of their commanders and their boldest knights, including their terrible reputations. He made the whole thing up, his madness fuelling his imagination so that he saw everything he described, even though Sancho could observe none of it.

"Hang on a minute," said Sancho incredulously, "how do you know this isn't more wizard's business? I can't see any knights over there, just a load of dust."

"Can't you hear their marching feet," shouted Don Quixote, "their fearsome war cries and the clanking of their weapons?"

"No," answered the squire. "It sounds like sheep to me, thousands of them."

"It's you who's a sheep, Sancho," laughed the knight. "But I am Don Quixote de la Mancha, and today I will make my name immortal."

He kicked his horse into action, and, with his lance levelled, he rode straight into the confusion of dust. Suddenly the cloud lifted and Sancho could see his master flailing about in the middle of a huge flock of sheep – just as he had guessed.

"They're not knights," he shouted after Don Quixote, "they're fleecy not fierce."

But our hidalgo still thought he was in the middle of a great battle. He began skewering the poor woolly animals on the end of his lance, and as soon as the shepherds saw their flock being savaged, they ran over and began raining stones down on the attacker. A rock smashed into the side of Don Quixote's cheek with such force he was knocked to the ground.

"Master," called Sancho Panza, hurrying over on his donkey.

"Those dastardly enchanters," mumbled Don Quixote through a mouthful of blood and chips of tooth. "They've done it again."

The shepherds and their sheep passed by on the plain, leaving Don Quixote to curse the wizard who had robbed him of his glory - and lost him four of his best teeth.

Knight of the Long Face

In which the quest continues, featuring an ogre, a gold helmet and some fellows who are felons

Don Quixote and Sancho Panza rode away from the scene of their skirmish with the sheep. Soon they entered a lush meadow set at the foot of some hills.

"This looks like a good place to rest for the night," said the squire, climbing down from his donkey and opening the saddlebags. "I'll have dinner ready in a jiffy. And breakfast and lunch... all rolled into one."

"Oh, Sancho," groaned the dejected knight. "How can you think of food, at this moment of my greatest despair?"

"When it comes to eating," replied the squire, "I say, 'seize the day'. Get it while you can, get it hot and in the pot, pronto. Anyway, what's all this grumbling about?"

"The loss of half my ear and a few brace of teeth saddens me, squire."

"I'm not surprised. At this rate there'll be nothing left of you in a week or two."

"My wounds are grave indeed," nodded Don Quixote.

"But I've never seen a man look more miserable," added Sancho. "We should call you *Knight of the Long Face*, because the priest told me that the knights in the story books are always named after their looks, some adventure or the style of their dress. And you look so long-faced, your chin is almost scraping the ground."

"Thank you, squire," replied the knight, recognizing his servant's insight. "It is an excellent title for such an unhappy knight as myself."

"Eat, and you'll feel better," Sancho declared.

"Food won't lift my spirits," cried Don Quixote, while Sancho started munching on bread and salami. "I feel that my courage hasn't been proven to the world. That cruel enchanter robs me of every chance for glory, and makes my task all the harder. We live in an age of corruption, greed and low ambition. Only by strength and chivalry can we rescue Spain from the rot. I must double my efforts to do good deeds and right wrongs - wherever I find them - and then perhaps I can save my country."

"You can start right here with the good deeds," Sancho screamed, tugging on his matted hair in sudden grief. "A terrible wrong's been done. I've opened the saddlebag where I keep our drink, and the wine jug must have been broken in the battle with the sheep. It's cracked and we've lost every drop of the scarlet reviver. And I'm as thirsty as a pharaoh."

"I have already told you," said Don Quixote calmly, "that knights can do without luxuries like alcohol. I will be happy with water."

"That's gone too," replied Sancho. "The leather pouch was torn in the fracas."

"It was quite a fusillade of stones," replied Don Quixote, rubbing his swollen cheek. "We must find a stream."

"That shouldn't be hard," answered the squire, saddling Rocinante and his donkey. "There's bound to be one nearby, to nourish all this grass. If we look over the hill we should find it – before it gets too dark to see."

But it was an hour before they heard the sounds of a waterfall or a fast flowing river up ahead, and the sun had already slipped over the horizon. Finding their way along a narrow track in the twilight, the two companions entered a thick forest of gnarled, old trees.

"The water's getting louder," Don Quixote noted.

"It's not just water," Sancho replied in a squeak. "Can't you hear that other sound?"

Don Quixote tilted his head and listened to the roar in the trees. He could just make out a thudding boom and the clank of iron, mixed in with the wind and the crash of water.

"What is it?" he asked the squire.

"I don't know, but I don't like it," replied Sancho.

By now, his teeth were chattering and his knees knocking together in fear. When he looked over his shoulder, he almost choked in terror. The path behind them had disappeared. They were in a clearing, ringed by tall, sinister trees, and it was rapidly getting dark.

"We're lost," he sobbed. "And that noise is growing louder every second. It sounds like some monster moaning."

Don Quixote raised his lance. "Yes, Sancho. It is an evil din, almost certainly the groans of some terrible, supernatural beast hunting for his supper. I confess that even my heart is quaking, but only a little. However, I am the proud Knight of the Long Face, and tonight I will at last prove my bravery to the world. Here is the challenge I need to establish my reputation. Whatever manner of fiend or ghastly ogre is stalking us in this enchanted forest, they will rue the day they tangled with my lightning lance."

"Ogre?" sobbed the squire. "Enchanted forest? Oh crikey."

"Wait here for me, my loyal Sancho. If I have not returned within three days, ride home to our village and tell my lady I died doing my duty as a good knight errant."

"Three days?" spluttered the squire, tears streaming from his eyes. "I can't do it. If you leave me alone one second in this place I'll die of fright."

"Pull yourself together, Sancho. A knight must never show cowardice."

"But I'm not a knight," yelped Sancho. "I'm allowed to be nervous. Think of my family, master. They'll never see their poor Panza again."

"I must go, my friend," repeated Don Quixote solemnly. "I ask you again to be brave enough to wait, just three short days, for my return. I hope you will not fail me."

Sancho Panza had realized that all his pleading wouldn't prevent his master from riding off to do battle with the ogre, so his mind was racing with devious tricks and schemes. It was now so dark he was able to move around without Don Quixote seeing him. He slipped off his donkey and looped a rope around Rocinante's hind legs, binding them together.

"What magic is this?" boomed Don Quixote as his horse refused to budge when he applied his spurs. "I'm stuck fast."

"It's that decanter again sir," squealed Sancho.

"Enchanter, you buffoon," roared the knight, furious that his battle with the ogre might have to be postponed.

"Perhaps this is a blessing, sir. It would be much safer, I mean, braver, to wait for dawn before facing whatever monster is making that racket. And if you kill the creature in the dark, nobody will be able to see what you've done, or record it in the history books."

"You have a point," said Don Quixote, grumbling. "My horse is frozen by the enchanter's mischief anyway. Perhaps at first light I can free her from his spell."

They spent that night shivering in the clearing, with the wind howling and the terrible hammering noise crashing through the trees. Sancho Panza stayed at his master's side, too scared even to remount his donkey. As dawn began to soften the black canopy of the sky, the squire slipped the rope from Rocinante's legs and stuffed it inside his tunic.

"I am free," cried Don Quixote, as Rocinante staggered forward. "Wait three days for me, loyal squire."

"Not likely," shouted Sancho Panza. "I'm coming along too."

Don Quixote set off between the trees with Sancho following, tugging his donkey behind him. The terrible sound was still ringing in their ears and, as the pair made their way through the wood, it got louder and louder. At last they came out into another clearing, where a cliffside waterfall fell into a pool. To one side of the pool stood some ramshackle huts.

"It's coming from in there," gasped Sancho Panza, hiding behind Rocinante's rump. Don Quixote advanced, fearlessly. As he rounded the huts he saw that the cause of the terrible noise wasn't an ogre or monster at all, but only some rusty old machinery clanking away under the power of the waterfall.

"It's a mill," cried Sancho Panza, peering around his master. "All night long we've been scared witless because of some silly little mill."

He fell to the ground and started rolling in the grass, hooting with hysterics.

"Stop laughing," ordered Don Quixote sternly.

But Sancho was fit to burst with his honking and gurgling. He laughed until he couldn't breathe, paused to catch his breath, then started up again.

"Squire," barked Don Quixote. "Stop your giggling at once."

"An ogre you said," Sancho spluttered between chuckles. "Rescue Spain from the rot, you said. Old Knight of the Long Face, we've spent the last six hours trembling..."

"I was not trembling," snapped Don Quixote, raising his lance.

'Trembling... because of a water feature," finished the squire, breaking into a rib-tickling bellow. Don Quixote rapped him twice with his lance, hard enough to make Sancho see stars.

"Don't doubt my bravery, you snivelling squire. I was ready to do battle with any monster, and would have done. We won't mention this again. Understood?"

"Understood," said Sancho, rubbing the spot where the knight had whacked him. But he was still

giggling when they rode away from that place, several hours later.

The Knight of the Long Face was more miserable than ever after his latest failed adventure. But once the sun had reached its highest point in the sky, he saw something ahead that made his heart soar.

"Look, Sancho," he cried. "Do you see that rider coming?"

Sancho was still sore where Don Quixote had walloped him, and had been thinking to himself that the life of a squire was too much like hard work and perhaps he'd be happier at home in a soft bed with a full belly. But he squinted at the horizon, wondering what his master had spotted.

"I see a man on a donkey," he told Don Quixote.

"That knight on a fine stallion," the knight corrected, "is Horatio the Brave, and his helmet is the most precious on this Earth."

"How do you know that?"

"I have read it in my story books. The helmet is unbreakable and the craftsmanship of its maker is unsurpassed."

"Well, he's got something on his head all right," said Sancho. "I think it's a barber's basin."

"It is a solid gold, battle helmet," cried Don Quixote. "That old proverb, *Every Cloud Has a Silver Lining*, must be true. Here I was, in the deepest pit of despair, after the doomed adventure in the woods..."

"You mean the adventure of the rusty machinery?" chuckled Sancho.

"Silence, squire, unless you want to feel my lance across your back. Yes, I was busy lamenting that adventure, and the fact that I didn't even have a proper helmet to protect my last good ear. And now I see Horatio riding across the plain, with the finest helmet in Christendom resting on his brow. I will challenge him and win it."

Don Quixote spurred Rocinante into a charge and bore down on the startled rider.

"Surrender the helmet, Horatio," he called out, "or I'll run you through like a shish kebab."

"But I am only a barber," pleaded the man on his donkey. "I have no helmet, only this brass basin I use for my work."

"If it is a basin, why are you wearing it on your head?" asked Don Quixote, reining Rocinante to a sudden stop.

"It was raining," answered the barber.

"You expect me to believe that?" scoffed Don Quixote, drawing his sword. The horrified barber jumped down from his donkey and took to his heels, leaving the basin behind him, rolling in the dirt. Sancho had ridden over and he scooped the helmet up and examined it.

"A good quality basin," he declared.

"Nonsense," barked Don Quixote, snatching it from his squire. He dropped it on his head and spun it round. "The visor is missing," he said.

"It's a basin," said Sancho, rubbing his eyes to make sure he wasn't mistaken. "I'm sure of it."

"Quiet, please. Someone has tried to melt the gold

down and damaged the visor, that is all. I shall wear it with pride."

So Sancho, remembering the bruises from Don Quixote's lance, buttoned his lip. He rode behind the knight, staring at the basin rocking on his balding head, trying his best not to giggle.

That afternoon they turned around a bend in the road and rode straight into a line of a dozen men, all linked together with heavy chains fastened around their necks. Their hands were bound with thick rope and their clothes were no better than rags. Four soldiers herded them along, cursing and lashing them with whips.

"Convicts," said Sancho Panza, "off to work the king's oar."

"I do not understand you, squire," said Don Quixote, studying the panting men, staggering towards them. "These poor wretches are prisoners?"

"They are, and they have to march all the way to the ocean," answered Sancho. "And once there, they will slave away in the galleys for a few years, roped to their oars."

"So they are being held against their will?" asked the knight.

"You could put it like that," replied Sancho.

"Then it is my duty to rescue them."

"Master," gasped the squire, "let sleeping dogs lie. Look before you leap, and all that. These are the worst thugs, dragged out of the deepest, darkest prisons. They must pay for their crimes."

"Squire, I am a knight errant, and my sworn mission is to serve the needy and those in distress. These men are friendless and in pain, just the sort of people I'm supposed to be helping."

As he was speaking, one of the soldiers ran up and asked him what was his business, to be blocking their way on the road.

"Move aside there," commanded the soldier, "and let the chain gang pass."

"I want a word with these men," Don Quixote replied.

The guard looked the knight up and down, and decided he must be going to a costume party somewhere, in his tin suit and with a basin perched on his head.

"Make it snappy," he growled. "We have a long

way to go."

Don Quixote rode along the line of breathless desperadoes, asking each one of them about his sins. The first man had stolen a tub of clothes and been sentenced to three years at the oars. The second was a horse thief and was facing six years. Each man questioned had a similar history of bad luck and harsh punishment, and Sancho Panza was moved to tears by some of the stories he heard.

"Why is this man wearing more chains than the rest?" Don Quixote asked the guards, when he had reached the seventh prisoner in the chain gang.

"This is Pasamonte," answered a sergeant, "escape artist and master of disguise. He's as slippery as a sack of banana skins."

"What is his crime?" asked Don Quixote

"He's been sentenced to ten years for crimes too many and too terrible to mention. Worse, he's sworn to escape before we can reach the coast."

The man before them was handsome and well built. He had a proud and dignified bearing, still evident despite the yards of chains wrapped all around his muscular body.

"Pasamonte is my name," the man cried out. "And any fool who insults me will pay the price when I finally break these chains. But I am no coward. Lead on, sergeant of the guard. Let's all do our duty and make no fuss about it. I've been in worse scrapes than this one and escaped to tell the tale."

Don Quixote was moved by Pasamonte's brave speech. He turned to the sergeant. "I have heard enough," he said. "These men are vulnerable and needy, and as a knight errant it is my duty to offer them protection. I ask you to release them at once. If they are guilty of their sins, we will leave them to be punished by their God, and not the drum-beating slave-driver onboard some filthy, rat-infested galleon."

"This crazy fool in the costume has flipped his lid," the sergeant laughed, calling to the other soldiers and breaking into chuckles. "He's got a basin perched on his bonce, but he still knows our own business better than we do."

Don Quixote was in no mood for this insolence. He swung his lance so it crashed into the side of the sergeant's head and knocked him out cold. The other soldiers fell upon the brave knight, and it would have been a brief and one-sided battle if the convicts hadn't joined in. Pasamonte snatched the keys from the unconscious sergeant's belt and freed himself. Then he managed to release the two men next to him in the chain. When the soldiers realized they were outnumbered, they ran for the hills.

"My friends," cried Don Quixote to the ring of jubilant criminals, wiping the blood and sweat from his forehead. "I have given you liberty. All I ask in return is that you visit my lady, in the village of Toboso, and testify to my courage."

"He's crazy as a coconut," Pasamonte shouted. "Grab him."

The gang of villains stoned Don Quixote, Sancho and their mounts until they all lay sprawling in the dirt. Pasamonte sprang on the knight, whipped the basin from his head and smashed it on a rock until it was cracked and misshapen. After rummaging through the saddlebags on Sancho's donkey, he ran off, driving the other convicts before him.

Ten minutes later, Don Quixote came to, rubbed his aching head and cursed the ingratitude of the men he had rescued. Sancho brushed off the dust, got his master onto his horse and led the way towards some distant mountains.

"You've done it now, Knight of the Long Face," he grumbled. "We'll be wanted men. The Holy Brotherhood will be after us."

Wild Men of the Mountains

*How the knight's adventure takes new twists
and turns and leaves
everyone feeling somewhat dizzy*

Sancho Panza guided his master deep into the Sierra Moreno mountain range, reasoning that the wilder and lonelier the country, the safer it would be for them. The squire was looking for somewhere to hide. He was sure that the Holy Brotherhood, the dreaded highway police, would soon be hunting for the wandering do-gooders who'd freed the chain gang. The Holy Brotherhood had a reputation for violence and viciousness that made Sancho's knees wobble. As he climbed higher into the boulder-strewn valleys of the mountains, the tubby squire fretted about the danger his master had put him in. Then he was overcome by an even greater anxiety: perhaps Pasamonte had stolen all their food when he ransacked their saddlebags. Sancho ripped the bags open, and let out a sigh of relief when he saw that the supplies were intact.

"At least we won't starve up here," he called to Don Quixote. "There's plenty of grub. We'll be fine as long as the wolves don't get us. Or the bears. Or the bandits, for that matter."

But Don Quixote was too absorbed in the desolate mountain scenery to pay any attention to these concerns. This was just the landscape he had been longing to explore, in pursuit of his knightly duties: a vista of menacing crags, sheer cliffs and perilous paths. He felt sure that the region would be rich in wonderful adventures.

While he was lost in these chivalric daydreams, Rocinante paused and dropped her head to nose at something on the ground. Don Quixote looked down his horse's mane and saw a weather-beaten saddlebag lying between some rocks. The knight tried to lift the bag with the tip of his creaky lance, but it was too heavy. He called Sancho over to examine it, and when the squire had turned it over with his foot, all the time grumbling about the risk of disturbing sleeping scorpions and snakes, he let out a whoop of excitement.

"Look at this," he cried, bending down and pulling the rotten bag apart. "It's full of gold escudos."

"What else does it contain?" Don Quixote asked.

"Some fancy shirts and a tatty old notebook."

"Pass me the book," ordered Don Quixote. "You may keep the specie, squire."

"Keep the what? *Eat the peachy,* did you say?"

"The coins, squire. Money means nothing to me. They're all yours."

There was another squeal of delight from Sancho. He handed the notebook to his master and began stuffing the gold into a little pouch he kept hidden, deep in the secret folds of his paunch.

"A poet," exclaimed Don Quixote, as he flicked through the pages. "I am not in the least surprised. This is perfect country for poets to stroll about in, as well as knights and squires."

"He can't have been a very happy soul," said Sancho, looking around at the bleak mountain peaks, "if he liked it out here. Is he any good?"

"It takes one to know one," said Don Quixote, stuffily. "Fortunately, knights are gifted poets themselves."

"Why's that?" asked Sancho. "What's rhyming got to do with the life of swords and lances?"

"Knights do much more than fighting," Don Quixote explained proudly. "They are ambassadors for politeness and decency. I may be the quickest swordsman in Spain, but I also have a sensitive nature. When there are ladies to woo and wild valleys to wander in, my thoughts always turn towards the gentle art of poetry. I judge that this man is a fine poet. He has been unlucky in love, his lady has been horribly cruel and he has come here to die of his loneliness."

"He sounds like a right barrel of laughs," Sancho quipped.

"You don't understand poets," replied Don Quixote, shaking his head at his squire's ignorance. "They are rarely happy. Their sadness is their inspiration."

"Indigestion, more like," answered Sancho. "They walk around looking glum all day and all they come out with is a load of hot air."

Don Quixote was about to reproach his squire for his coarseness when he heard the crash of a rock fall behind him. Turning in his saddle, he saw a figure scampering across the bare hillside a hundred yards away. It was a man, naked except for some ragged velvet trousers, with filthy skin and long, matted hair. The man moved quickly, crouched almost on all fours, his bare feet knocking into the stones and sending them flying. With a mad cackle he disappeared behind the crest of the hill. Sancho crossed his chest.

"Lord protect us," he spluttered. "These mountains are full of demons."

"No, Sancho," said the knight. "I believe we have found the rightful owner of those escudos you have concealed so carefully around your belly."

"He can't be," cried Sancho, his chubby fingers closing around the hidden sack of gold coins. "That was a mountain sprite or a goblin, I'm sure of it."

"It was a man and, given the loneliness of our location, the chances are he is the broken-hearted poet we've been speaking of."

"It's not just his heart that's broken," whined Sancho. "His mind must have snapped. He was hardly wearing a stitch."

"We must find him and talk with him."

"Why do we want to do that?" stammered Sancho. "It's finders keepers, losers weepers around here, matey. He threw that gold away."

"We must follow and help him," replied Don

Quixote disapprovingly. "You circle around the hill on your donkey. I'll go the other way."

"I'm not going anywhere on my own," cried the squire. "Can't I ride behind you? I'll protect our rear."

They set off across the rocky slope, with Don Quixote tutting at his squire's greed and cowardice.

When they reached the other side of the hill, they found the grisly remains of a mule, stretched across a ditch.

"His steed," declared Don Quixote. "He must have left it where it dropped, dead from hunger or exhaustion."

"That's no way to treat an animal," replied Sancho, patting the side of his donkey. Sancho had many faults, but he did love his donkey.

"Quiet, squire," commanded Don Quixote, "do you hear that haunting melody?"

Before Sancho could answer, an old shepherd appeared from around the side of the hill, driving his flock before him with whistles and a soft singing. He was surprised to see the knight and squire on the path, but he raised a hand in greeting.

"I'm not used to strangers in these parts," he told them in a reedy, suspicious voice. "Are you friends of the wildman?"

"We saw someone on the hill," replied Don Quixote. "Was this his mule?"

"It was," answered the shepherd. "Did you see a discarded saddlebag, by any chance?"

"We did."

"I haven't touched it myself," said the old man, settling himself on a rock. "I don't want to get mixed up in anything... illegal, or worse. There are strange forces at work in these mountains. I wouldn't want to be cursed for taking another man's possessions. It's best to let sleeping dogs lie."

"Isn't it just," said Sancho cheerily. "You won't catch me poking my nose into any saddlebags, no sir. I wouldn't touch another man's saddlebag in a million years, wouldn't dream of it."

"What do you know of this wildman?" asked Don Quixote, interrupting his squire's prattling.

"About six months ago," the shepherd told him, "I was resting my bones at a camp we have on the other side of these mountains, when a handsome lad rode up on the very mule you now see dead before you. This boy asked for directions, to the loneliest part of the mountains. We told him to keep riding and he'd find it. The paths all end in this place, and you can go for months without seeing another human being."

"You're giving me the creeps, old man," Sancho blurted. "I bet you've told a few ghost stories around the campfire in your time, haven't you?"

"We didn't see any trace of him for weeks," continued the shepherd, ignoring the squire. "Then he started stealing food from our camps, attacking solitary shepherds and scaring our sheep. We tracked him down to an old oak tree, where he sleeps in a hollow in the trunk. Sometimes he is well-spoken and polite, but will never answer our questions.

Other times, he turns crazy, flies into a rage and tears around like a mad dog. Again, we can get no sense from him, though he repeats the same word over and over in a snarl – Fernando. I fear he is mad and nobody can save him."

"I am Don Quixote, Knight of the Long Face," cried the knight, striking his dented suit of arms with his fist. "It is my sworn duty to give aid to the unfortunate, and I pledge that I will scour these mountains until I find this wildman. I, Don Quixote, will save him."

"It won't be necessary to scour anything," shouted Sancho in a panic. "He's coming down the hillside right towards us."

The wildman was tottering towards them, his arms outstretched and his face contorted with pain. "You men," he cried in a desperate whimper, "have you any food for a hungry fool."

Don Quixote realized immediately that the man was close to starvation. He ordered Sancho to lay out a spread from the saddlebags and the four men sat down in the grass studying one another.

"I cannot thank you enough," said the wildman, diving into a chunk of salami and gulping on some wine. "There was a time when I only used the best silverware at my table. Now I must eat furtively and seldom, like a hunted lion or a lone wolf."

"I can see that you are from a good family," said Don Quixote confidently, "although your britches are torn and dirty, they are made of the finest velvet.

In addition, there is a scent of precious ambergris about you."

"You are wondering perhaps, how I came to be in this sorry state?" asked the wildman.

"I long to hear the explanation," replied the knight.

"Then the reward for this meal you have proffered is a desperate tale, told by a desperate man."

He ate for a few minutes in quiet concentration, then settled back in the grass and began his story.

Cardenio's Tale of Woe

In which the wildman spills the beans

"My name is Cardenio and I am from a noble family in the south of the country. Until six months ago, I really thought of myself as the happiest, and luckiest, man alive. The reason for my happiness was called Luscinda, my childhood sweetheart and my eternal love. Her beauty is flawless, unmatched by any other woman, and her kind nature is equal to her physical perfection.

"After long years of unspoken love, I finally approached Luscinda with my secret and was overjoyed to learn that she could return my passion. She had loved me for years but never dared to reveal it. We swore our loyalty to one another and I hurried to her father with my proposal. He received me like a son, but wanted the marriage offer to come from my own father, to make the match official. I rushed to my father's rooms, but found him reading a letter. It was from Duke Ricardo, one of the richest and most powerful dignitaries in Spain. He had heard good reports about me and wanted me to join his retinue, as an aide.

"You must serve the duke," my father told me. "It is too good an opportunity to miss." So, like a fool, I went to see Luscinda and told her we must delay our wedding so that I could see what the duke had in mind for me. I tried to be optimistic, thinking that perhaps, in a year or two, I would be rich and respected and in a better position to support my sweetheart. She was understanding and pledged her unwavering love.

"I rode off to the duke's castle the next day and within a few months I was running his estates. I enjoyed my work - though I was heartsick for Luscinda - and made many friends. One of these was the duke's own son, Fernando. He had a wild streak in him, and an eye for the ladies. Already, he had been embroiled in some scandal with a wealthy farmer's daughter that had set every tongue in the castle wagging. But, despite his reputation, I liked his company. When he asked if he could visit my father's house for a few weeks, while conducting some business in my town, I thought it was an excellent idea. I would escort him and have a chance to visit my beloved Luscinda at the same time. You see, gentleman, how incautiously I invited this sneaky viper into my own house.

"My greatest mistake was to tell him about Luscinda, how beautiful and desirable she was. In my lovesickness I talked about her endlessly, and always in the most flattering terms. Fernando pestered me for an introduction, and at last I allowed him to see her, a glimpse of her at her window. All he said afterwards was, "you have not lied." I never guessed that he had fallen in love with her, and decided then and there that he would steal her away from me, whatever the cost.

"But why haven't you married her?" he asked craftily, as we walked back to my house. "Does her father object to it?"

"I must talk to my own father first," I confided. "And since I have been working for the duke I haven't had a chance."

"Then I shall speak to him, on your behalf," Fernando assured me, "and ask him to arrange the wedding."

I was grateful at the time, and thought nothing of it when Fernando asked me to go away for a few days on his business. But on the third day I received a letter from Luscinda that almost stopped my heart from beating with shock.

"Fernando," she wrote, "has asked my father for my hand, and we are to be married, in a secret ceremony, in two day's time. Have you forgotten me, Cardenio? Why have you not come to aid me, to rescue me from this dastardly man?"

I ran to my horse and rode day and night towards my town. It was dawn on the day of the wedding by the time I arrived outside her house. I slipped in through a side door, found my way to the chapel and hid behind a tapestry. My mind was racing with rage and fear and my sword was ready in my right hand.

Before I had a chance to catch my breath, a priest entered, leading Fernando, Luscinda and her parents

in a solemn procession. My sweetheart wore a wedding dress of fine silk, white as fresh-fallen snow. I was so shocked at the sight of her in this gown, I lost track of what the priest was saying, but my ears pricked up when Fernando said, "I do," and all eyes turned on Luscinda, expecting her to reply. There was an agonizing silence while she hesitated. I was ready to jump out with my sword and slice my rival to shreds, but some terrible doubt held me back. I realized I was waiting to hear her answer, to test her love, to satisfy my pride.

"I will," she muttered and fell to the ground in a dead faint. I was so shocked by her words I couldn't move a step. Luscinda's mother stooped down and tried to bring her daughter around, while the other people in the chapel shouted for a doctor and ran about in confusion.

"There is a note in her hand," her mother cried. I saw Fernando snatch it away from her clasp, his eyes staring in horror at the words before him. But I was too overcome with despair to linger there any longer. Luscinda had thrown me away and so I came to these mountains to end my days as a wandering hermit, alone and unloved and beyond any person's help. This is how you find me, today."

As he finished his story he fell back on the ground and stared up at the sky, sobbing. Don Quixote, Sancho and the shepherd all glanced at each other, bewildered by the tale they had just heard. With no warning, Cardenio's heels started pummelling the ground, his body shook and foam appeared around his lips.

"He's having an attack of the crazies," cried the shepherd. "The story must have triggered it."

"Does he get violent?" Sancho yelped.

"You bet he does," replied the shepherd.

"Do not fear," said Don Quixote, getting to his feet, "you are safe with me at your side."

Cardenio was up in a flash, snarling and cackling with wild staring eyes. He flattened the knight under a blur of punches, then turned on Sancho and the shepherd, beating them black and blue. Don Quixote could only lift himself up on one elbow and squint under the rim of his cracked basin-helmet at the shape of Cardenio running away over the hill.

Flagellation and Flagons

Don Quixote makes a bold decision and the priest dons a dress

As soon as he recovered, Sancho helped his master to his feet and wiped the dust from his suit of arms.

"The quicker we get out of this place the better," Sancho panted. "We can ride down to the plain and take our chances with the Holy Brotherhood. It'll be far less risky than staying here. That Cardenio's mad as a stone."

"He is a good man," whispered Don Quixote through his bruised lips. "We have much to learn from him."

"Speak for yourself," said Sancho. "But I say he's a dangerous screwball, and I've got the bruises to prove my point."

"All great men go through a period of despair when they must question everything they believe in," answered Don Quixote, solemnly. "It is called 'the long, dark night of the soul' by some poets."

"Is it now?" replied Sancho. "I think I'd rather sleep right through mine if that's all right with you. I want to wake up for breakfast with a smile on my face."

"You will go at once," commanded Don Quixote, "to my mistress, Dulcinea." The knight drew himself up to his full height and fixed his squire with a steely gaze. "I am staying here in these mountains, to torment myself. Cardenio has set me an example and I will follow in his footsteps. You will take a message to my mistress and I will remain here, flagellating myself mercilessly until you return."

"*Flag-deflating?*" cried Sancho. "What's all that about? Is it painful?"

"Very," answered Don Quixote seriously. "I will apply the scourge without relief."

"What's he muttering about?" Sancho asked the shepherd, who was just stirring after Cardenio's frenzied attack. "What *urge* is my master suffering?"

"He's going to whip himself," the man muttered. "I swear, everyone I meet in these mountains is a raving loon."

"Squire," boomed the knight. "Stop wasting time. Fetch some paper and a pen and ink. I am going to ask Dulcinea el Toboso to put my mind at rest, once and for all."

"And where will I find a pen out here?" Sancho squealed.

"If there is no pen," answered the knight, refusing to be put off by such minor details, "then I will dictate my message for you and you must recite it, bending down dutifully before her, as soon as you reach her castle."

"Is it a short message?" asked Sancho. "Only, I've got a brain like a sieve."

"This is no time for your jokes," roared Don Quixote. "I am about to perform a duty of devotion to my mistress, out here in this barren wilderness, and I demand that my squire memorizes my heartfelt message, word for word."

"I'll try my best," Sancho replied in a whimper.

The knight paced around for a few moments, trying his best to compose a profound and moving message for his beloved Dulcinea. At last he grabbed Sancho by the ears and fired off a stream of words. It was a beautiful love poem, a noble and heartbreaking plea for the cruel Dulcinea to put his mind at rest forever. If she loved him, she must answer "yes" and loyal Don Quixote would ride to her at once and remain by her side for eternity. Should the answer be "no" he would wander forever in these dismal mountains, with only the wild goats, the wolves and the wind for his companions. It was a love poem to make even a flint-hearted hermit weep. The shepherd stared up at the knight, amazed by his creative skill and the conviction of his love. He would recite it to his friends around the campfire that evening. The words were etched in his mind, forever.

But Sancho had forgotten everything except "yes" or "no" - even before his master had finished speaking. The squire was too busy thinking about flagons of wine and pigs' trotters, and all the other scrumptious things he was going to sample as soon as he arrived at an inn. For a second he felt a pang of guilt for failing Don Quixote - but then he decided that, as long as he got the answer right everything would be fine.

"Ride quickly, Sancho Panza," ordered the knight, pushing the squire towards his donkey. "Look after Rocinante for me. I have no need of my horse or any other comfort. My ordeal must begin immediately and will not cease 'till I have my answer."

Sancho watched open-mouthed as Don Quixote extricated himself from his iron suit and tore off his vest and trousers. The knight picked a rock from the ground and smashed it into his naked chest. Then he snapped a branch from a dead tree and began lashing himself with it, all over.

"Don't overdo it, Don Quixote," Sancho screamed. "Otherwise there'll be nothing left of you before I'm out of the valley."

"Get moving, squire," answered Don Quixote. "And don't spare your donkey's hide the whip."

Without another word the knight was running up the hillside, pausing now and again to scourge himself with the branch, bash himself with the rock, and pledge his undying love to his mistress, between terrible cries of pain.

Sancho Panza rode out of the mountains on his donkey, leading his master's horse. He followed the highway across the plain until he came to an inn. As he climbed down from his donkey, rubbing his belly in preparation for the feast he was hoping for, the village priest stepped through the door. He and the local barber were riding to a nearby town on business and had stopped at the inn to water their horses.

"Hello, what have we here?" said the cleric.

"Hello, Father, how are you?" was Sancho's response. "How's the food in this place?"

"Never mind that," snapped the priest sharply, waving to the village barber who was saddling the horses. "Didn't I hear that you'd taken a job as squire to my troubled friend, Señor Quixano?"

"That is my new profession," answered Sancho proudly. "I serve the Knight of the Long Face in the squirely capacity."

The priest shook his head in dismay. "Don't tell me you've been taken in by this knightly nonsense, Sancho? You do realize that poor Señor Quixano has lost his marbles?"

"There have been a few strange things happening," said Sancho, scratching his chin. "And he is a bit unpredictable. But the prospects for squires are excellent, so I'm sticking with it. Don Quixote tells me I'll soon be the governor of my own island. Now, if you don't mind, I've got an appointment with a flagon of wine and a plate of hot grub inside the tavern."

"Stop where you are," commanded the priest. "Where is your master?"

"He's on secret business," replied Sancho, tapping the side of his nose mysteriously. "I wouldn't reveal his location even if I was tortured for weeks."

"But those are his saddlebags," said the barber, who had joined the two men and was listening to the conversation. "And didn't I see you leading his horse behind your donkey?"

"Perhaps you've killed our friend and stolen his possessions," suggested the priest calmly. "Do you think we should call the Holy Brotherhood?" he asked the barber.

"He's in the mountains," said Sancho. "He's got the urge."

"I beg your pardon," replied the priest.

"I mean, he's got the *scourge*. He's bashing and lashing himself until he's all cut to ribbons. I'm to ride to his mistress with a message and bring her answer to him. Otherwise he'll roam forever in the wilderness."

"Her answer to what?"

"Something about love."

"I see," said the priest. "He's paying penance."

"*Pens*, no we couldn't find any *pens*," said Sancho, trying to be helpful.

"Be quiet, you knucklehead," answered the priest. "It's time we brought our friend Quixano home and soothed his crazed mind. We need a plan of action."

"I agree," said the barber. "There must be some way we can entice him to return to the village."

"All this talk of knights and squires has given me an idea," replied the priest.

"Where do we start?"

"Well, we're both going to need a dress..."

Later that day Sancho led his donkey out of the stables, escorting two large ladies on the road to the mountains. The women looked uncomfortable riding sidesaddle on their mounts and their make-up was rather sloppily applied, to say the least. But when you understand that this was the priest and barber in disguise, it all makes perfect sense.

The priest knew that the mad knight was armed and dangerous and there was a chance he would resist any attempts to escort him back to the village. With this in mind, he'd devised an ingenious plan. He and the barber would impersonate a princess and her governess - they had to be in disguise or the knight would recognize them instantly.

After an awkward conversation with the innkeeper's wife, the priest had persuaded her to part with her two finest dresses. She thought it was a strange request and was only prepared to surrender the costumes in exchange for the priest's cassock, which she would hold as security until his return. The next stage of the plan was to make Sancho Panza lead them to their friend and lure him out of the mountains with a chivalric challenge.

"What challenge?" asked the barber, trying to stuff his long beard inside the top of his dress.

"Our kingdom is threatened," replied the priest. "An ogre, no, ogres are too small, a fierce giant has invaded our lands and he's going to eat my father, the king. We've been told Don Quixote is the bravest knight in Spain and we have come to beg him to help us save my father."

"It sounds crazy," said the barber.

"Precisely," responded the priest. "He's so nuts he might just believe it."

"Can I be governor if we defeat the giant?" asked Sancho Panza greedily.

By dusk they were high in the forbidding landscape of crags and cliffs of the Sierra Moreno. They made camp by a little stream and Sancho prepared a hearty snack of hard cheese, offal and blood-red wine.

"I have a question," he told the priest, once he was munching on a hunk of bread. "It's about your plan."

"Fire away," answered the cleric. "Questions can only make good plans stronger and bad plans weaker, and it's better to know which of the two we're dealing with."

"It's about the scourging," said Sancho. "If my

master Don Quixote thinks I didn't do my duty with the love message to his lady, he'll whack me with his lance."

"A good point," replied the priest, musing on the problem. "You must tell him you saw his lady and she wants him to come at once."

"If I tell him that, he'll race to the village," said the squire. "Then you needn't bother him with your giant problem."

"Let's hope so," cried the priest, clapping his hands in delight. "You will go at first light, Sancho. With any luck we won't have to embarrass ourselves in these ignoble disguises."

In the morning Sancho went off in search of the knight, while the priest and barber – still in their disguises – washed in the stream and made themselves some breakfast. Their bacon was sizzling away in the pan when Cardenio crashed into the camp and fell down in the grass before them.

"Good ladies, I haven't eaten for two days," he blurted. "The sound of your frying pan was tormenting me, and though it shames me to ask, may I take breakfast with you?"

At first, the sight of the wildman alarmed the barber and the priest, but they remembered the story Sancho had told them around the campfire the night before. At the time they had discounted it as more squirely fantasy, but now they realized it must have been true.

"My poor Cardenio," said the priest. "You are

welcome to join us and take some comfort in this harsh prison you have made for yourself. We are already acquainted with your sorry tale." And he quickly explained who they were and the nature of their business in the mountains.

"Thank you, Father," the wildman replied, after listening patiently. "They say I have fits of madness from time to time, but my mind is at rest at this moment. I will try my best to control myself in your presence."

The three men sat down to their meal and the priest asked Cardenio gentle questions about his family and his likes and dislikes, before the events that led up to him becoming a recluse.

"I know you mean well, Father," said Cardenio, "by making me remember my loved ones and all that life has to offer outside these cold mountain ravines. But I am beyond help, believe me. My heart has been torn apart and can never be healed. Not even a miracle could rescue me from this miserable life I am condemned to."

As Cardenio was speaking these words, the priest heard a soft singing, coming from behind some boulders across the stream. He raised his hand to silence Cardenio and the three men stood up and walked over to the edge of their camp. It was such a beautiful voice and such sad words, they were drawn towards it like bears to honey. After paddling across the stream they stepped around one of the boulders and saw a boy dressed in peasant clothes, sitting under a tree. He was singing a sad love song and slowly unbuttoning his tunic. The priest didn't want to interrupt the singing, so he indicated to the others that they should duck down behind some nearby rocks. The three men watched as the boy stood up and laid the tunic across a branch of the tree. He slipped off his shoes and walked down to the water to wash himself, singing all the time.

"Look," whispered Cardenio in amazement, "his feet are white as marble."

"They certainly don't look rough and worn like a peasant's," added the barber.

The men gasped when the peasant boy removed his cap and folds of flowing blond hair dropped down his back.

"It's a woman, I believe," said the priest.

"And almost as beautiful as Luscinda," added Cardenio.

"We must show ourselves at once," ordered the priest and the men stepped out from their hiding place.

The girl screamed when she saw them and made a dash across the rocks, but the sharp stones along the bank were too much for her delicate feet. She slipped and fell to the ground.

"Do not fear us," the priest shouted. "I am a man of the cloth, this is my friend the barber and this other man is a nobleman."

"He looks more like a bandit than a Don," cried the girl. "And if you are a priest, why are you wearing that dress?"

"That's a long story," answered the priest, with a sigh. "But we have a fire blazing on the other side of these boulders and lots of food. If you will accompany us I will be pleased to tell you all about it, in more comfortable circumstances."

"I accept your offer," she replied humbly.

"Good," said the priest warmly. "Because I would also love to know why you're wearing a tunic."

A Princess Arrives

*Another tale of woe: the plot thickens
until it almost sets*

Each man fussed around the new guest sitting at the fire, offering her blankets, cups of wine and all the other small luxuries Sancho had hidden in his saddlebags. The priest quickly explained how he was in the mountains to aid his old friend and asked if she had seen the mad knight in her travels.

"I have been wandering in these hills for months, kind sir," she answered. "Although I've seen many incredible things, I haven't come across any lunatics in metal suits."

"But why do you stay here?" Cardenio asked her. "This is no place for someone so fair, so beautiful as yourself."

"It is my beauty that has brought me to this sad situation," replied the girl despondently. "Beauty is no guarantee of happiness. My story would draw sobs from a stone."

"Then you must tell us everything," demanded the priest. "It is my business to hear problems and attempt to solve them." He leaned back against a tree-trunk, looking as calm and composed as he did at confession, even in his dress and amid all that wild mountain scenery.

"My name is Dorotea," the girl began. "My parents are wealthy farmers in the state of Andalucia..."

"But that is my home state too," Cardenio gasped.

"Don't interrupt," barked the priest. "Please be silent until the tale is told."

"I could not have been happier with my life," Dorotea continued. "Even though I had to work hard, managing my parents' crops and animals, we were a very close family and I didn't want for anything. My days were satisfying but busy. There was little spare time to go out riding or visit my few friends in the town. But, despite all this, I was spotted by a prowling predator, a low snake by the name of... Fernando."

Cardenio gulped so loudly Dorotea looked up in surprise. The priest shot him a reproving glance and nodded for her to go on.

"This rogue was the son of the duke who owned my parents' estate. I had never met a man with his charm and passion for life. When he promised to marry me, I confess I was overwhelmed. Although I knew he was a bit wild, I had fallen in love and was determined to transform him into a respectable husband. My parents were so excited by the match, they mortgaged our farm and borrowed heavily from the banks to provide a dowry and an extravagant wedding for their only child. But on that terrible nuptial day my dear Fernando revealed his true nature. He ran away to another town, abandoning me at the altar. My father led me into our village church weeping with joy, and led me out with tears of anger and disgrace burning his cheeks.

"I am not the kind of woman to let a man shame me and my family so easily. Once I had helped my parents save our farm from ruin, I rode after Fernando, accompanied by a loyal manservant. I was determined to make the cad marry me, help him become a better man and rebuild my life.

"But, as I entered the town to which he'd fled, a crier was swinging his bell and telling the news of a strange and scandalous wedding that had taken place that very morning. I listened in horror as I heard Fernando's name mentioned. It seems he had fallen in love with a local girl, Luscinda, and persuaded her parents to make her marry him.

But Luscinda was in love with another man, some Cardenio, and in the middle of the wedding ceremony she had fainted in despair. She had said "yes" to the marriage vows, but only because she could not bring herself to disobey her parents. Her true feelings were revealed in a letter she was carrying in her hand, in which she confessed that she had already pledged herself to Cardenio. This letter was made public by Luscinda's maid, who was in her confidence. She wrote that she was planning to stab herself with a dagger at the first opportunity, if Cardenio did not come to rescue her before the wedding to my Fernando was completed.

"As if these events had not been chaotic and heartrending enough, the town crier had much more to tell. Apparently, the priest dissolved the wedding at once and my flighty husband rode off on his stallion in a rage. Cardenio disappeared, leaving a note saying he was sure to die of his loneliness and despair, while Luscinda ran away from home searching for her true love.

"I really didn't think it could get any worse," said Dorotea with a sob, "but the next piece of news was the posting of a reward for my capture. My father thought I'd eloped with my trusted manservant and that this secret love affair was the reason for Fernando's absence at our wedding.

"The news drove me almost out of my mind. Not knowing what I was doing, I rode out to hide in a lonely forest, where I was promptly robbed of my horse and purse by bandits. For weeks I wandered the countryside, too shamefaced to go home, too sad to think of starting a new life for myself. I ended up in these mountains. They seemed the perfect place for me to weep away the rest of my miserable days."

The three men sat in silence for several minutes, too shocked by the tale of Dorotea's adventures to utter a sound. Then Cardenio jumped up from the grass and clambered onto a boulder. "A miracle," he yelled, waving his arms at the sky. "She still loves me."

"Who does?" asked Dorotea.

"Luscinda," answered the priest. "Allow me to introduce you to Cardenio."

"Is it possible?" gasped Dorotea. "But that means

they can still be married."

"I don't see why not," replied the priest.

"And Fernando could still be mine?" she added.

"Perhaps I can have a word with him," said the priest kindly, "on your behalf. I'm sure I can make him see sense."

And they all laughed and cried and danced around in jubilation, except the priest who didn't think it was appropriate for a man of the cloth to get too hysterical.

"Now that things are looking rosier for you two," began the priest when the group had calmed down a bit, "perhaps we can get back to my friend, Don Quixote."

He quickly explained the situation, and his plan, and Dorotea and Cardenio both pledged their help.

"I don't suppose you've read any stories about knights have you?" the cleric asked Dorotea.

"Hundreds," she answered. "Reading was one of my only entertainments out on the farm. I always wanted to be a fairy tale princess."

"I'm certain you'd make a better 'princess' than I could. Do you think this dress would fit you?"

As soon as Dorotea had left the camp to change into her costume, Sancho Panza appeared over the crest of the hill, red-faced and wheezing. The instant he saw Cardenio he darted behind the priest's back.

"It's the wildman," yelped the squire. "Is he in one of his rages?"

Cardenio bowed and explained to Sancho that he was a changed man. "I no longer wish to be a hermit," he said with a laugh. "My crazy days are finished."

"That's all well and good, but I'm still aching where you thumped me," answered Sancho, rubbing his blubbery physique all over.

"Sancho," snapped the priest, "stop your whining and tell me about your master."

"I gave him the message. But he's not ready to show himself in front of his lady. He says he's got more scourging to do first."

"As I suspected," replied the priest. "He's probably enjoying it too much. Let's hope he's willing to help the princess."

Sancho scratched the top of his head. "The princess with the giant problem?" he asked.

"The same."

"Well, I've been thinking about that," said Sancho proudly. "I think this whole princess business is something you've made up. You were even wearing a dress when I left the camp, as a disguise. There never really was a princess, was there?"

"Oh yes there was," cried Dorotea, stepping out from behind the boulder and looking every inch a royal damsel in distress. Not only did she manage to look beautiful and stately in the innkeeper's wife's scruffy dress, but her cheeks were streaked with tears as though she had been weeping for her threatened kingdom.

"My friends," she pleaded. "We cannot stand here

and debate the point. Every moment we delay brings greater peril for my poor father."

"Does it?" blurted Sancho, ready to start blubbering himself he was so moved by her appeal.

"Squire Sancho," she continued, in her best regal voice, "is the Knight of the Long Face ready to serve me?"

"I'm afraid he's busy right now."

"Nonsense," cried Dorotea. "My need is greater than his present ordeal. You must take me to him at once."

A few minutes later the whole camp was loaded onto the donkeys and Sancho knelt down on the ground so Dorotea could mount Rocinante from his shoulders. The priest and the barber slipped into long robes that hid their faces and Cardenio had a shave in the stream. He looked like a new man. When the priest was happy that none of them would be recognized, he gave the order to depart.

Don Quixote was standing in the middle of the next valley, lashing himself with his scourge, the gnarled and twisted branch of an old olive tree. The moment Dorotea spotted the crazed hidalgo, she urged Rocinante into a canter, dismounted next to the knight and threw herself at his feet.

"Good sire," she cried, between impressive sounding sobs, "will you hear my plea? Is it true that you are the indomitable Don Quixote, renowned rescuer of trembling unfortunates and last hope of all fair maidens in distress? If so, lend me your lance, my lord. I have a terrible challenge for you."

"Arise, my lady," said Don Quixote, offering her his hand. "From your fine dress and impeccable speech, I can tell you have royal blood coursing in your veins. It is not seemly for highborn ladies to bow down before knights."

"Alas, I cannot rise," she sighed, "until you agree to offer me the services of your invincible sword arm. I have been riding for weeks, searching everywhere for you. A giant ravages my lands and threatens to devour my father..."

"An outrage," boomed the knight. "Your father is off the menu, rest assured."

"Then will you accompany me to my kingdom, to do battle with this villain?"

"Of course," replied the knight, soothingly. "I am not the world-respected warrior and chivalric daredevil, Don Quixote, for nothing. I'll cut this giant down to size in a jiffy."

"Will you promise to come at once, and to refuse all combat until the challenge is completed?"

"I will," answered the knight. "My noble lady, Dulcinea el Toboso, must understand that I cannot refuse princesses in distress. Your case must take priority – even over hers. I will resume my scourging as soon as I have slaughtered your giant. Now arise, or I will die of shame to see you humbled before me any longer."

Dorotea sprang nimbly to her feet. "Sancho Panza," she called, "bring your master's suit of arms. We are leaving immediately."

They rode out of the valley and down from the mountains that same morning, a long procession of strangely dressed pilgrims voyaging across the naked Spanish plain in silence.

Homecomings

More lucky meetings and some white-faced demons

Late in the afternoon, the group arrived at the same inn where the priest and barber had intercepted Sancho. The innkeeper ran out to greet them and the priest quickly bustled him to one side.

"My friend in the iron suit is mad as a March hare," he whispered. "He thinks he's a knight."

"My wife said something about a lunatic roaming the roads," replied the landlord. "The Holy Brotherhood has been asking after him."

"He's harmless really," the priest explained. "But I thought it best to warn you so you don't put your foot in it later. Give us rooms and a fine dinner and I'll make sure you're well paid for your trouble. We will leave at first light."

"The knight has to sleep in the loft where I keep my wine," answered the landlord sternly. "I don't want him breaking anything if he goes daffy. And I'm short of space anyway. Half my stables are piled high with hog cages. A swineherd is storing them here, ready for market day in the next village. And a servant passed through earlier to make a special reservation for four rooms."

Once the animals were fed and watered, the guests enjoyed a dinner of stewed lamb shanks and mashed turnips. Don Quixote poured the wine from a chipped jug, with all the solemnity of a king hosting a state banquet. It was late when they all tumbled off to their beds, and most of them were already snoozing by the time an ornate carriage pulled up at the inn. Three men in fine clothes climbed out through its velvet-curtained doors, followed by a tall woman dressed in a white satin robe. They hurried inside and went straight to their rooms.

Long after midnight, the priest was awakened by an odd gushing sound, as though a river had burst its banks. He sat up in his bed and lit a candle. There was a scream above him, then a huge crash. At once, the whole building was ringing with shouts. The door swung open and Sancho Panza fell into the room, covered in blood and gasping for air.

"My master is fighting the giant," he whinnied. "It's a bloodthirsty battle up there."

The priest rushed over to the squire and helped him to his feet. "But Sancho," he cried, tasting his fingers, "this isn't blood on your clothes."

"It's giant blood all right," Sancho squealed. "Be careful, it might be enchanted."

"It's wine, you simpleton," replied the priest and he pushed past the puzzled squire and sprinted up the stairs to the loft.

The priest shuddered when he saw the scene

before him. Don Quixote was thrashing around with his sword, stabbing at some huge pigskin sacks suspended from the ceiling. With each sword thrust, a spurt of the innkeeper's wine cascaded onto the knight's head.

"Another deadly wound," called the knight in triumph, as the wine soaked him and blinded his eyes. "Soon there'll be no blood left in your body and victory will be mine."

Before the priest could decide what to do, the innkeeper dashed into the room and wrestled the knight to the floor.

"Don't move a muscle, you dunderhead," he roared at Don Quixote. "My wife's sent for the Brotherhood. You'll pay for this damage, every last centavo of it."

"Get off me, you knave," cried the knight. "Can't you see I'm vanquishing a giant? I woke in the night and saw him looming above me, his ugly skin shining in the moonlight."

"That's my best vintage, you vandal," replied the innkeeper, staring in dismay at the wine gushing across the wooden floor. "Let's get you downstairs."

He wrestled the protesting Don Quixote to the door and dragged him along the stairway. The priest followed, pleading with the innkeeper to forgive the unbalanced hidalgo. With the innkeeper's shouts, the priest's entreaties and Don Quixote's sword banging at every step, the whole inn rushed to the hallway to see what was happening.

Cardenio popped his head around a door, rubbing the sleep out of his eyes. Across the hallway, the woman in the satin gown asked her escort why she had been disturbed.

"I know that gentle voice," Cardenio shouted.

"Who's that?" called the woman, rushing into the hall.

"Luscinda," cried Cardenio, his eyes filling with tears.

"My Cardenio," sobbed Luscinda, hurrying to his arms.

"Come back here," growled Luscinda's escort, following his mistress into the hall. But now Dorotea stepped out of her room.

"Fernando!" she screeched, "it's you, you rogue."

"Dorotea," the man moaned. "Oh darling, I can explain everything."

"Nobody move," roared a man in a uniform, stepping into the hall. "I'm from the Holy Brotherhood."

"Oh crikey," gasped Sancho, creeping into the kitchens.

It took an hour of questions and tears before everyone settled down enough for the priest to take control of the situation. He began by reuniting the duke's son with his bride-to-be and reminding him of his Christian responsibilities. Next, he handed over ten gold escudos to the innkeeper and his wife and soothed them with kind and moving arguments about the 'chivalric sickness' that afflicted his poor friend. As for Cardenio and Luscinda, they were too busy staring into each other's eyes to trouble anyone. Only Don Quixote and the officer from the Holy Brotherhood were still flushed with anger: Don Quixote, because he was convinced that his old foe the enchanter had transformed the giant into a wineskin, and the officer, because he suspected the knight might be the same fruitcake who had liberated a dozen dangerous criminals from the chain gang, only a week earlier.

"This castle is enchantcd," roared Don Quixote. "Who are all these people? And why is this thuggish man pointing at me?"

"I am an officer of the law and you're under arrest," replied the officer.

"You can't arrest a knight, you buffoon," laughed Don Quixote. "Knights are models of virtue and above the law. The king will hear of your rudeness."

"Of course he will. You can send him a letter from prison."

"Any more cheek from you," snarled the knight, "and I'll chop off your head."

"I'd like to see you try it. And I've got five men outside to back me up."

Before they could come to blows, the priest stepped between them.

"Gentlemen," he cooed softly, "this is no way for us to behave in the company of ladies."

"I agree," said Fernando, resting a hand on the officer's arm and leading him to one side. "My wife-to-be has explained the situation," he whispered, "and I don't want this poor man arrested."

"Oh really," answered the officer, shrugging off Fernando's hand. "And who might you be?"

"I'm the duke's son."

"Then of course I am at your service, sir. But I can't just leave this crank to wander around causing mischief, can I? He needs treatment of some kind."

"Perhaps the priest has a suggestion?" said Fernando, turning to the cleric.

"Tell your men to rub chalk on their faces," the priest told the officer, with a smile on his face. "And leave the rest to me."

"Brave Don Quixote," called Dorotea from her room, ten minutes later. "Grant me an audience, will you?"

"At once," cried the knight and he stepped into her chamber.

"You have saved me from the giant, my noble warrior."

"I regret," replied the knight, "that while we were engaged in violent swordcraft, an enchanter turned him into a wineskin, my lady."

"It does not matter," said Dorotea with a warm smile. "He was in his death throes when the evil enchanter flew by on his magic carpet. The giant is no longer a menace to my kingdom. You are free to leave now, good Don Quixote, having completed my challenge."

"It gave me great pleasure to serve you, princess," said the knight, with a tear streaking his weather-beaten cheek.

"And I will never forget you for your good deed," Dorotea answered. "Now, it is almost dawn. Go to your valiant steed and get questing again."

Don Quixote collected his metal suit and weaponry from the loft, summoned squire Sancho from where he cowered in the kitchen and marched out into the courtyard. He was just fixing the cracked basin on his head when eight ghostly figures surrounded him and dragged him to the mouth of a wooden cage, mounted on a cart. They wore black capes and their faces were white as bone.

"In you go, knight," the demons hissed. "Our enchanter master is sending you on a journey back to your village."

Don Quixote struggled for all he was worth, but he was no match for the enchanter's minions. They tossed him into the cage and tied the door shut with some twine. Then they strapped Sancho to his donkey, roped its halter to the bars of the cage and opened the courtyard gates.

"Your friend, the village priest, is passing on the highway," the demons cackled. "He will guide you home."

One of the demons – in truth the officer from the night before – took the reins of the cart and drove it out to the road. There the barber was waiting to replace him in the seat. The demons ran back to the inn, turning to wave farewell to the priest, because among them were Cardenio and Fernando – and it is only polite for friends to wave farewell.

The priest had arranged the whole ruse, and Don Quixote could only groan at the audacity of his opponent, the enchanter, as he rattled along the dusty track that led to his village.

"But I suppose I have reasons to be cheerful," the knight said with a sigh, "despite my imprisonment."

"What are they, then?" cried Sancho, who was still none the wiser about the deception and was mourning his lost position as a governor of an island.

"We have had some adventures together, squire," replied Don Quixote, "the like of which no common man will ever experience. And we are lucky that our good friends the priest and the barber happened to be passing, because I like their company."

"That's so," agreed Sancho. "And I have the hundred escudos, safe in my money–belt. My wife will be sure to give me a smile when she sees them glinting in my hand."

"All in all," the knight continued, "our adventures have been glorious. I have no idea what is to come, but I am sure it will be just as thrilling."

He closed his eyes and drifted off to sleep, as the cart creaked its way homeward, across the scorched scrubland of La Mancha.

Part Two

Riding Out Again

In which the knight makes a startling discovery that gives him itchy feet

For two weeks our demented hidalgo lay sprawled in his old four-poster bed, sleeping away the days and mumbling through the nights. His niece and housekeeper watched him like a pair of hawks, trying their best to keep his mind off dungeons and dragons, giants and enchanted castles. In the third week, the señor was sitting up on some pillows and accepting soup and water. By the end of a month, his eyes were clear and he was showing signs of his old, sensible self. He talked lucidly and calmly about politics, the arts and the business of his property and savings. His carers rejoiced and sent a message to their master's old friends, the priest and barber, to inform them he was healed. They came to pay Don Quixote a visit that same morning.

"Old friend, you look well," said the priest, settling into a chair at the knight's bedside.

"I'm fully recovered," Don Quixote replied. "Indeed, I'm brimming with energy and anxious to get back to my old life."

For twenty minutes they chatted and joked like old times. Don Quixote impressed the priest with his wisdom and insight: he had plenty to say about the affairs of Spain.

"So where do you stand on this new warning from our king?" the priest asked seriously. "There are whispers that the Turkish sultan is sending a great navy to plunder our shores."

"I would like to give the king some badly-needed advice," answered the señor.

"And what qualifies you to give advice to the monarchy?" inquired the barber with a mocking grin.

"All men are entitled to an opinion," the knight replied. "If the opinion is worthy and well-considered then it deserves to be heard, even by royal ears. A man's status in life should be no reason to show him disrespect. If his mind is clear and capable enough, every man should have the right to address his rulers."

"Well said," cried the priest. "I couldn't put it better myself in my morning sermon."

"So what clear and capable advice do you offer?" the barber continued.

"I have a simple plan for defeating the sultan altogether."

"It must be a brave and ambitious plan," said the priest.

"It is. The best plans always are."

"So will you tell us what it is?" asked the barber, growing impatient.

"With pleasure. I would summon all the knight errants in Spain to a meeting in Madrid and hold a great joust to decide who was the bravest amongst them. Then I would send the victor into the field against the Moorish horde and watch as he single-handedly conquered the sultan's combined armies. One valiant knight could easily handle twenty thousand ordinary soldiers. If the king would agree to this, the whole problem with the Saracen menace would be over by lunch time."

"Oh dear," sighed the niece, who had been eavesdropping at the doorway. "It looks as if Uncle's gone loopy again."

"I fear, señor," sighed the priest, "you are still in the grip of these knightly delusions."

"You can say that again," added the barber, watching Don Quixote demonstrating the necessary sword thrusts to dispatch the sultan's armies, while still sitting upright in his bed.

"Perhaps this cure of rest and recuperation is not the right approach," the priest whispered to the barber. "We might require more shocking tactics to return our friend to his sanity."

There was a sudden, ear-piercing howl from outside and the priest almost jumped out of his socks. A moment later, the niece darted in.

"It's Sancho," she cried, tugging on the priest's cassock. "He's trying to force his way inside."

When the priest and barber reached the courtyard they saw the housekeeper and Sancho Panza locked in combat. The chubby ex-squire was getting the worst of it.

"Take that,"shrieked the housekeeper, delivering another terrible blow to Sancho's ample belly. "How dare you ask permission to visit Señor Quixano? It was you that encouraged my master to go off pretending to be a knight."

"You've got the wrong end of the stick,"Sancho whimpered, bent over in pain. "It was me that was deceived. He promised me an island. Anyway, I have important news to give him."

"Be quiet, both of you," ordered the priest. "Let him in, señora. I can't imagine how he can make the situation any worse. And besides, I need to speak to you and Don Quixote's niece in private and at once."

Sancho squeezed past his opponent with a huge grin on his face. The others huddled in the shade of an almond tree, discussing the patient, and leaving the squire to climb the stairs and make his report.

"A book, you say?" boomed the knight.

"That's what I've heard."

"What kind of book?"

"I don't know all the details," answered Sancho. "But last night I was at a party to welcome young Carrasco back home. He's been studying at Salamanca University and has just finished his degree. Before I could open my mouth to say "hello" he told me he'd read all about the windmills you thought were giants, the magic basin..."

"It's a helmet."

"...and the chain gang fiasco..."

"And that was no fiasco," Don Quixote snapped. "It was a noble deed."

"...and all our other adventures and some I don't even remember us having. He said the book is called *Don Quixote* and it's selling like hot cakes."

"Does this Carrasco fellow live in our village?"

"He does."

"Then bring him to my bedside, squire," the knight instructed. "I want to hear everything he knows on the subject of this strange publication."

Sancho returned a few minutes later, leading a young man with a pudgy face and impish expression into the room. Before Don Quixote could speak a word, the youth prostrated himself in front of them.

"Oh great knight, I am humbled to be in your most eminent presence."

"So I see," replied Don Quixote. "If it's true that a book has already been written describing my adventures, it must be a flattering one."

"It is indeed true," answered Carrasco, getting to his feet. "And in all the histories of chivalry, nobody can find a braver or more extraordinary knight than Don Quixote."

"Is it popular with the reading public?"

"The book is adored by every man and woman in every social class, by professor and pupil, rich and poor alike. It has even provided people with new expressions in our language. So, for example, when two girls see an old, scrawny nag trotting past, one might joke, "there goes a right Rocinante." Everybody loves you and Sancho, your characters and conversations. I've even heard the old boys in taverns debating which of your adventures was the finest: the battle with the sheep, the seizing of the magic helmet or the lashing in the mountains."

"A difficult choice," agreed Don Quixote, scratching his chin. "All of those adventures were daring and risky."

"There are a few criticisms as well," Carrasco added awkwardly. "Some readers believe you drift around a bit, rather aimlessly..."

"Knights do not drift," roared Don Quixote. "They roam, and that is the proper way for any knight to behave."

"There are also some missing details," Carrasco went on. "The hundred escudos Sancho pilfered..."

"What do *pilchards* have to do with this?" cried the squire.

"The money you took from the wildman's saddlebag," explained Carrasco. "What became of it?"

"Never you mind," Sancho barked. "If it wasn't for that loot my wife would have thrown me out on my ear. She wasn't happy with me drifting all over the country, you know."

"*Roaming*, Sancho," the knight corrected.

"I don't care who's *foaming*," Sancho bleated. "My family deserved every penny."

"Quiet, squire," the knight commanded. "Carrasco, if this book is so popular, docs it mean the author has prospered...financially?"

"He must have," answered the student. "There is even talk of him writing a sequel: *Don Quixote PART TWO*."

"The cheek of it," squealed Sancho. "I suppose he thinks he can just rush out some new adventures without asking us first. But we'll show him. We'll go out on so many new adventures and battles and giant wallopings he won't know where to start with his scribbling."

"Well said, squire," cried Don Quixote, hopping out of bed. "It's high time I was back in the saddle again. My public needs me."

"Don Quixote rides again," cheered Carrasco, trying to control his giggles.

"He will," said the knight proudly, "in a week's

time, when we've made our preparations. You are cordially invited to wave us off, Carrasco."

"I don't know what Teresa my wife will have to say about this," mumbled Sancho, sheepishly. "She says I'm a blockhead for doing so much work and getting so many bruises, all for the promise of an island kingdom."

"But it was your idea in the first place," Carrasco laughed.

"I got a bit carried away," replied Sancho.

"Have no fear, squire," said the knight in a soothing voice. "This time I'll put you on wages. Any islands I decide to grant you will be considered a bonus. As for you, Carrasco, I ask you to keep our intentions secret."

"You have my word as a scholar."

"I thank you," replied Don Quixote. "Now, if you will excuse us, we have our plans to make for the quest ahead."

The student shook hands with the knight and his beaming squire then rushed down the stairs to the courtyard. Then he hurried over to the almond tree and told the priest everything that had happened.

A Joust in the Forest

Dulcinea gets a makeover and Don Quixote proves his mettle

On the evening of the seventh day, Don Quixote and Sancho Panza saddled their trusty mounts and got ready to ride out onto the plain. Carrasco shook their hands before they left, wishing them good luck with their questing. As the three men chatted in the courtyard, the housekeeper and niece burst out of the house and screeched like alley cats.

"What's going on? Where is the priest?" demanded the niece. "He should be here to stop this madness."

Carrasco took her to one side, while the housekeeper berated the knight and his squire for their foolishness.

"I'm acting on the priest's advice," Carrasco whispered to the niece in a conspiratorial hiss. "You will understand our tactics in a day or two."

"This had better work," spat the niece. "Uncle's making a laughing stock out of us all."

Don Quixote interrupted their whispers with a shout of farewell. Then Carrasco opened the hacienda gates and the questing duo departed on their mission for fresh adventures.

"So what's our first move?" asked Sancho, when they'd been riding for an hour.

"It is not proper," replied Don Quixote sternly, "for squires to ask such questions of their masters. Indeed, I would prefer it if you kept conversation to a minimum."

"But I'm a Panza," Sancho protested. "We love to banter."

"I had noticed. Knights, however, prefer to ride in silence."

"But if I don't talk," said the squire, "I get hungry."

"You are an unconventional aide de camp, squire Sancho."

"I don't care for the sound of that. But I know what I am and I've no intention of changing."

"Well, if you must know my plans," the knight said wearily, "we are riding to El Toboso where you will guide me to the palace of my mistress. Too many months have I passed in chivalric duty, and still never gazed on the lady I serve."

"Crumbs," cried Sancho. "Now I wish I'd never asked."

"What was that?" snapped Don Quixote.

"I mean, oh dear," the squire mumbled, "I'm not sure I know where she lives."

"You delivered my message to her, didn't you?"

"Of course I did."

"Then lead the way. El Toboso is only ten miles

from here. We'll be there long before nightfall."

Much later, the squire and his master were riding around the dark streets of El Toboso, hopelessly lost.

"It might be down this one," said Sancho, gesturing towards the mouth of a dank alleyway. "Or that one, over there," he cried, pointing into another.

"Squire," said the knight coldly. "I cannot believe my mistress lives down some revolting alleyway. We are looking for a stately palace, not a hovel. Now where is it?"

"My visit was a long time ago," Sancho answered desperately. "Be patient, won't you?"

"All night long we've been getting nowhere, and it is now as dark as the inside of a cow."

"I'm sorry, master. I can only suggest we ride out of town to make camp for the night. In the morning I should be able to find your mistress easily."

"I agree to your suggestion," sighed the knight. "But do not fail me tomorrow, or you'll feel the sting of my lance across your rump."

After a hearty breakfast, Sancho left Don Quixote waiting in their camp in a grove of chestnut trees and ambled towards El Toboso. "I'm in a right pickle," he sobbed. "I'll lose my wages when the knight finds out I've tricked him. It's all that do-gooder priest's fault. If he hadn't stopped me at the inn, I would have visited the master's lady."

Then he remembered Dulcinea was only a peasant girl, and that neither he nor the knight had ever met her. He sobbed even louder. There was no princess to be found, whatever he did.

While he was trying to think of a solution to his troubles, he saw three peasant girls riding across the meadow on donkeys.

"For all I know," he said to himself, "one of those rough-looking country girls could be Dulcinea." Then he slapped the top of his head. He was having an idea and it was making his brain hurt. The next second he had turned his donkey around and was racing back to the woods.

"Don Quixote," he cried, "master, I bring great news."

"Will she grant me an audience?" panted the knight, straightening his beard in an effort to improve his appearance.

"Polish your suit," Sancho replied. "The princess couldn't wait to see you. She's riding over with two maids."

Don Quixote ran around in a panic. Sancho helped him into his iron suit and, only minutes later, the knight was atop Rocinante, cantering through the trees.

"But Sancho," he cried, when he'd ridden into the open, "there is nobody here to greet me."

"Over there, sire," the squire replied. He pointed at the peasant trio who were riding past.

"All I see are three ugly girls on donkeys," said Don Quixote.

"But sir, those are the three prettiest women I've ever laid eyes on. Their horses are Arabian stallions and each maiden wears the finest, golden velvet clothes."

"No, squire," answered the knight. "I can see nothing of what you describe."

Sancho kicked his donkey in the ribs so hard it bolted forward and blocked the path the girls were taking.

"Dulcinea," he called to the first girl. "Don Quixote awaits you." He reached over and grabbed the reins of her animal.

"Out of the way, tubby," laughed the girl. "We've no time for any horseplay."

Don Quixote had dismounted and was creeping forward through the grass on his knees. "Are you my mistress, princess?" he asked the girl softly. "Are you Dulcinea, the sweetest rose in Spain."

The girl let out a raucous laugh, blasting the knight and squire with her bad breath and garlic fumes. "Sorry, Granddad," she hooted, "I can't waste my time chatting with lunatics."

She gave Sancho such a hard kick he almost fell off his donkey, and the three girls sped past Don Quixote leaving him in a cloud of dust.

"Vile enchanter," moaned Don Quixote, tearing at the grass. "He has changed my true love into a coarse and repulsive country wench."

"It's a disaster," cried Sancho, clapping his hands in glee because his plan was working so well. "She's been switched."

"Truly I am the Knight of the Long Face," sobbed Don Quixote. "The enchanter strikes me in my weakest spot, despoiling the one I am sworn to serve. I must find a way to break his spell and restore her beauty."

"That will be a proper adventure," said Sancho trying to stifle a giggle.

"Lead me back to the woods, squire. I am weak with grief and need rest before our quest can begin."

Don Quixote spent that day lolling in the woods, reciting poetry about lost loves and broken hearts. Sancho had less lofty things on his mind. He raided the saddlebags and devoured two salamis and the contents of a leather bottle of wine. As soon as the sun dipped below the treetops, he closed his eyes and began to snore.

"Sancho," Don Quixote suddenly hissed. "I can hear two men approaching, stalking in the forest."

The squire flicked his eyes open in panic and crawled over towards his master. "Where?" he gasped.

"On the other side of those bushes."

Before the knight could utter another word, a firm voice echoed around the wood. "Squire, pass me my lute. I must compose a love song for my lady."

"Gadzooks," whispered Don Quixote. "It's another knight errant. I thought I could hear his weapons clanking."

"It will be a sad song, of course," came the voice. "Because, although my lady, Casilda, is the most beautiful in Spain, she is also the most hard-hearted."

"This knight lies," snarled Don Quixote under his breath. "No woman can hold a candle to my Dulcinea. When she's not enchanted that is."

"Maybe he doesn't know about Dulcinea," whispered Sancho, who was eager to avoid any trouble with the strangers.

"And she has sent me, the Knight of the Forest, on my mission," came the voice, ringing around the trees, "to vanquish all knights who deny my claim for her unparalleled beauty. This task vexes me, but it is her cruel nature to demand it."

"Yes, my lord," said a squeaky voice. "It vexes me too."

"That must be his squire," whispered Sancho. Don Quixote shushed him at once.

"But now that I have defeated the renowned Don Quixote," said the Knight of the Forest, "and forced him to accept that his Dulcinea is no match for my Casilda, my task is almost done. Don Quixote was the bravest of knights and now he's been thrashed there are few who will dare to argue with me."

"You are mistaken," cried Don Quixote, stepping out of the bushes. "Here is a knight come to challenge you."

"I cannot see you, stranger," replied the Knight of the Forest. "This forest is too gloomy. May I request your name?"

"It is Don Quixote."

"Impossible. I left Don Quixote bruised and battered in the field of battle, only two days ago."

"I do not know the identity of your opponent,"

said Don Quixote proudly. "But he was an impostor. You must be careful in this country. There is an enchanter at large who plays tricks on careless knights. You have been deceived. I am the true knight of La Mancha, and I say that Dulcinea is the most beautiful lady on the face of this earth."

"Then we shall do battle," the other knight replied coolly.

"At dawn, we joust," spat Don Quixote.

"There is one condition," added the Knight of the Forest.

"Name it."

"The loser must return to his village and swear to remain there and not enter into any combat, for a period of one year."

"I accept," cried Don Quixote. "If I could not defend the good name of my lady, I would be ashamed to carry my sword."

As the first glimmer of dawn broke over the woods, Don Quixote was waiting in a clearing, his lance at the ready. The Knight of the Forest appeared on the far side of the enclosure, sitting on a nag almost as worn-out as Rocinante. His metal suit was scuffed and dented and, mysteriously, he had already lowered his visor. But this sight was nothing compared with the appearance of his squire. Sancho watched in horror as his opposite hobbled out from among the trees. The man was hunchbacked and gnarled. His twisted figure was wrapped in a black cape and the cloth hid everything except a portion of his face. On this face was the most enormous nose Sancho had ever seen. It was bright purple, bloated and fat, at least six inches long and covered in revolting warts and black spots.

"Look at that conk," Sancho gasped. "Have you ever seen the like?"

"It is an uncommonly unpleasant snout," the knight agreed.

"Sancho Panza," said the ugly squire in his squeaky voice. "It is a hard life serving a knight, is it not?"

"It is indeed," said Sancho nodding.

"When our masters joust, we are expected to fight too."

Sancho couldn't take his eyes off the purple nose. The idea of it brushing against him sent a shiver running down his spine.

"I'm not the fighting kind," Sancho whimpered.

"We'll see about that," said the other squire, raising his knotty fist and shaking it in Sancho's direction. "When this is over you'll realize that you'd be better off at home looking after your wife and family."

Sancho was too terrified to answer. He hurried after Don Quixote, who was positioning Rocinante for the charge. Without any warning, the Knight of the Forest kicked his horse in the ribs and advanced at a trot. Don Quixote immediately spurred Rocinante into a near-gallop and came bearing down on the other knight.

Sancho didn't wait to see the outcome of the

joust. He ran to the nearest tree and scrambled up into the branches, while the squire with the purple nose taunted him below. On the field of battle, the Knight of the Forest suddenly paused. His horse neighed and refused to take another step, unhappy with all the kicking he was getting. As the knight fumbled with his lance and tried to get his mount moving, Don Quixote thundered across the clearing and smashed his opponent out of his saddle. The Knight of the Forest landed in an undignified heap and bellowed in pain. Don Quixote was by his side in a flash, his sword ready at his throat.

"Do you yield?" he demanded.

"I do," wheezed the Knight of the Forest. "I'm all broken up."

"Sancho, remove his helmet," ordered Don Quixote.

Sancho Panza dropped down from his tree and sprinted past the shocked squire of the purple nose. He flicked the defeated knight's visor up with the toe of his sandal.

"Well I never," he cried. "This knight looks just like that student fellow from the village, Carrasco."

"So he does," agreed Don Quixote. "The power of this enchanter to alter human features is amazing."

"No, I really am Carrasco," the student sobbed.

"It might be safer to finish him off, sir," said Sancho. "One less enchanter would be one less thing to worry about."

Don Quixote raised his sword and Carrasco gulped. But before the blade could fall, the squire of the purple nose ran over and dragged the student to safety. Next he whipped off his cape, then his nose, and standing before them, there was the village barber.

"Amazing," said Don Quixote. "This enchanter never stops."

"No, I'm the barber," said the barber, pointing at himself. "Put your sword away."

"What about the nose?" asked Sancho.

"Papier maché."

"Get me to a doctor," sobbed Carrasco. "He's cracked my ribs."

"I thought you said you could ride," said the barber angrily, dragging Carrasco back towards their camp. "The priest is going to be hopping mad when he finds out about this."

"A victory of sorts," sighed Don Quixote, watching the two men vanish into the woods. "But this enchanter is growing stronger all the time, Sancho. Nobody is safe from his face-swapping trickery. We must find a way to break his spells. Break camp, squire, we ride at once."

Then he left Sancho alone in the clearing, scratching his head and trying to make sense of everything he'd seen.

Wild Beasts and Magic Ships

The Don stares danger in the face and Sancho gets cold feet

"This is the life," said Don Quixote. "There's nothing better than questing, Sancho. We're free as mighty eagles, soaring above the clouds."

They were riding through lush fields of wheat, the sun was warming their backs and the smell of wild flowers hung in the air. Don Quixote was elated after his victory over the Knight of the Forest. He didn't suspect for a moment that it was all a plot by the priest to bring him back to the village.

Carrasco and the barber had agreed with the cleric that as it was chivalry that was driving their friend insane, so the laws of chivalry should be used to cure his madness. If Don Quixote was bound by his own word to stay in the village and give up questing, his recovery would be certain. But, thanks to Carrasco's bungling, Don Quixote had emerged the champion. The encounter only made the deranged hidalgo feel more confident in his knightly abilities.

"I'm still a little confused," said Sancho, scratching his head. "What if that knight really was Carrasco?

And perhaps the purple-nosed monster was truly the barber."

"Nonsense," snapped Don Quixote. "What would our friends be doing creeping around in those woods, dressed in those ridiculous costumes? And don't doubt this enchanter's skill. Have you forgotten how easily my poor Dulcinea was transformed?"

"That's just the point," Sancho replied. Don Quixote took this to mean that the squire shared his opinion. But Sancho knew that he was responsible for the Dulcinea face-shift mystery. This made him question what was true and what was fiction. He was still fretting when they crested a low hill and saw in the distance a cart approaching. Its bodywork was decked with ribbons and flags, the mark of royalty.

"Look, squire, a fresh adventure is already speeding our way."

"But that's one of the king's carts," Sancho spluttered. "We mustn't interfere with it. Remember the chain gang."

"Knights never interfere," Don Quixote roared. "But it is my duty to investigate all strangers and their cargoes."

He kicked Rocinante into a trot and moved into position, blocking the road. As the cart approached, the two men on the driving board began waving and shouting at the knight and his squire. "Get out of the way. Sling your hook. We're on official business."

"Halt, or I'll slice you in two," answered the knight, raising his lance. "I demand to know what you carry."

"Lions," called one of the men, fixing the brake on his cart. "An African prince is sending a pair of them as a gift to our king."

"Are they big lions?" asked Don Quixote.

"Huge," answered the man.

"Dangerous?"

"Thirsty for blood they are. I've been dealing in lions for years and I've never seen anything like these beasts. What's more, they're starving because we haven't fed them today. And when they're hungry, they get even more vicious than usual. So clear off, old tin suit, before you get scratched."

"Don Quixote isn't scared of any pussy cats," replied the knight. "Open their cages. I will face these ravenous monsters, armed only with my sword."

The men started gurgling and hooting with laughter. "He's fresh out of the funny farm is this one," said one of them. "Enough joking now," said the other, "off you go before you get hurt."

Don Quixote swung his lance so its razor-sharp tip hovered only an inch from the driver's nose. "Open their cages," he repeated.

"But, master," screamed Sancho, who had peeked in the back of the cart. "I've just seen a claw sticking out of this crate and it was as long and sharp as a two-foot dagger. These are real beasts, not the enchanted variety."

Don Quixote never turned his stare from the driver's face. "If those cages aren't open in one minute," he hissed, "I will remove your heads quicker than my squire can chop a carrot."

"That's pretty fast," Sancho added.

"I think he means it," the driver told his mate. Then he spoke to the knight. "At least let my friend ride away to safety with our mules, before I release the lions."

"I grant your request."

"Can I go too?" squealed Sancho.

"Yes, squire," replied Don Quixote, shaking his head. "If I do not survive this adventure, take my remains to the enchanted peasant girl and explain to her who she is and who it was that loved her."

"That might be a bit messy," said Sancho. "What if they eat you?"

"Sancho, you are a buffoon. Take Rocinante with you and wait for me at the top of the hill."

The squire didn't hesitate and the driver's mate followed him, cantering up the slope on their mounts. Don Quixote slipped to the ground, armed only with his shield and sword, and paced around to the rear of the cart. There was a deep, rumbling growl from one of the cages, loud enough to make the boards shake.

"Will you reconsider?" asked the driver, who was hiding at the back of one of the cages. "Once I pull this rope the door will fall open, and your life will come to a very sudden end."

"Don Quixote does not flinch from danger," cried the knight. "Pull away."

The door flapped open with a crash and an

enormous lion stuck his head into the air. His jaws were black and covered in thick drool; his teeth were yellow and curled and sharp as scissors; his eyes flickered and blazed as though on fire.

"I'm waiting for you, king of the jungle," cried Don Quixote fearlessly. "Are you too scared to come out?"

Standing there in his cracked iron suit, the old hidalgo looked spindly and feeble. But he was staring death in the face. The driver watched in awe as the knight taunted the lion. "You old flea-bag," cried Don Quixote. "Drive him on, keeper. Hit him with a stick."

The lion glared at the knight, only a few feet away from his great black nose, then turned around in his cage and sank down to go to sleep.

"This lion is a coward," cried Don Quixote. "Rattle his cage and make him roar."

"I will not," replied the driver, fixing the door of the crate back into place. He jumped down to the ground and bowed to the knight. "You are the bravest man in Spain. Nobody else would dare to go up against such a man-killer. And if your opponent will not face you in combat, you are the winner of the contest."

"Will you swear this to our king?"

"He will receive a full and glowing report of your incredible bravery."

Don Quixote signalled to Sancho that it was safe to return. When the squire had recovered from the shock of finding his master in one piece, Don Quixote ordered him to give the driver two escudos from the saddlebags. This was to compensate the men for the delay to their journey.

"From this day on," he announced, "I wish to be known as the Knight of the Lions. Men will tell tales of this adventure for hundreds of years to come."

The squire and the driver and his mate all cheered the gallant knight. Sancho celebrated by opening some wine and it was close to dusk before they were on their way again.

The Knight of the Lions and his squire found shelter that night under a huge elm tree. At the break of dawn they rode down into a lush valley and by noon they were standing on the banks of the River

Ebro, admiring the view.

"This great cataract must flow all the way to the sea," Don Quixote sighed, staring across the wide river. "What a fine adventure it would be to float out onto the ocean waves."

"I don't know about that," Sancho grumbled. "All you get to eat on those sailing tubs is hard biscuit and salt beef, for months on end."

"You would be a better man, squire, if you could forget your stomach occasionally," replied the knight.

"But I'm very fond of it," cried Sancho. "We go everywhere together."

Don Quixote was about to rebuke his servant when he saw something bobbing in the shallows, between some trees. He rode over and discovered a small boat, tied up to the bank. "A magic ship," he whispered to himself. Sancho followed and watched as his master dismounted and untied the craft.

"What are you up to?" the squire asked. "Some fishermen will be back for that any minute."

Don Quixote chortled. "Don't be a fool, squire. If you had studied chivalric history, as I have, you would know that when a knight stumbles across a ship, or other mysterious method of transportation, it is always an invitation to be carried to another kingdom on some adventure."

"Mysterious?" said Sancho. "It looks like a plain old fishing boat to me."

'Tie the horses to that tree, squire," ordered the knight. "Then climb aboard,"

"Is it safe?"

"Perfectly safe," snapped Don Quixote. "With me at the helm, you have nothing to fear."

Sancho gingerly approached the fragile boat and tested its bottom with one foot. He swung his weight and flopped down on the boards. Don Quixote pushed the craft away from the bank and a current caught them in an instant, pulling them into the deep water.

"Where are the oars?" asked Sancho.

"Magic ships don't need oars," answered the knight, confidently. "That's why they're magical."

"But we're being pulled into the rapids."

And so they were.

"Magic ships travel at incredible speeds," explained Don Quixote, calmly. "Knights are transported between kingdoms in a matter of seconds. That white water you can see foaming all around us is a sure sign that we're rapidly approaching our destination."

"We're rapidly approaching something," shrieked the squire, staring over the prow. "It looks like a water mill."

"That will be an enchanted castle," said the knight, getting to his feet and almost flipping the boat over. "Our adventure must be to rescue a maiden or kidnapped king held captive there."

"It's a water mill and we're heading straight for the wheel channel," squealed the squire. "We'll be crushed to splinters."

Sancho started paddling desperately while Don Quixote licked his lips with excitement.

"Look at that," cried the knight. "Those white-faced demons are attacking again."

The millers, their faces covered in flour dust, had seen the boat rushing towards the mill and run out onto the landing around the wheel.

"Turn the tiller, you maniacs," one of them shouted. "You're being sucked into the channel."

"Release the maiden, you rascal," the knight called back, waving his sword over his head. "We know she's in there. And we're not scared of any wheels."

Every second, the boat rushed closer to the great clanking buckets of the water wheel. Two of the millers ran inside and came back carrying a long pole. They tried to push the boat away from the channel.

"They've armed themselves," cried Don Quixote.

"But my sword is mightier than their lances."

Sancho covered his eyes with his pudgy fingers, expecting any second to be ground up by the water wheel. But, despite Don Quixote's parries with his sword, the millers managed to flip the boat over and steer its occupants away from the channel. Don Quixote's metal suit dragged him straight to the bottom of the river, but the old hidalgo could swim like an eel and he made it to the bank. He landed in the grass and flopped there like a stunned fish. Sancho slammed into the planks of the landing and was dragged out of the flood by the angry millers. They slapped him about a bit then rowed him to the bank to join his half-drowned master.

By the time Don Quixote had coughed a few gallons of the river out of his system, two hefty fishermen were standing over him, clenching their fists.

"Where's our boat?" asked one of them, not too politely.

"Those demons capsized it," replied the knight, struggling to his feet. "It was a short adventure but a wonderful one. I was caught between two warring enchanters. One of them transformed your humble craft into a magic ship, the other changed it back again."

"He's cuckoo," said one of the fishermen.

"We want damages," said the other.

"My squire will pay you for the use of your boat." Don Quixote pointed at the bedraggled Sancho being hauled onto the bank. "He carries my purse."

The two men stomped over to the squire and after a very short conversation, Sancho handed them four gold escudos. When they'd departed he approached the knight, shaking with cold and every bone aching from the beating he'd received.

"I suppose you want me to fetch your horse?" the squire barked.

"A good idea," answered Don Quixote. "The sooner we leave, the sooner we reach our next adventure."

Sancho limped along the riverbank, cursing the day he'd agreed to come out questing with this cracked hidalgo. He was tired of sleeping under the stars, eating half-rations and risking his life in these madcap japes. What's more, the purse was getting so light he was beginning to wonder if he'd ever see any of his promised wages.

The squire mumbled and groaned all the way back to where Rocinante and the donkey were grazing. "Perhaps, Sancho mate," he muttered, "it might be time to retire."

The Flying Horse

*The Knight's reputation precedes him and
Sancho meets the cat of nine tails*

For three days Sancho grumbled and sulked in his saddle, while Don Quixote led them deep into a thick forest. Their food was almost gone and the squire had to go to sleep hungry, curled up in a damp blanket, with one eye open for wolves and other predators. But, instead of trying to find them shelter and provisions, the knight was proud of their sufferings. *A hard life makes a brave heart*, he kept reminding Sancho. The squire thought he'd rather have a soft pillow and a well-stocked larder than all this hardship. But each day they pushed further into the leafy wilderness.

At sunset on the fourth day, they entered a clearing and saw a group of riders emerging from the trees on the opposite side. One of them was a lady dressed in green velvet, sitting on a white charger. She had long golden hair and she sported a falcon on her right forearm.

"A huntress goddess," gasped Don Quixote. "Or perhaps even a princess? She will certainly want to make my acquaintance."

"Oh really?" Sancho replied with a smirk. "Your eyes are full of that enchanted dust again. She's probably just a rich farmer's wife who wants us to mind our own business."

"Ride over there and introduce me," answered the knight, ignoring his squire's jibe.

"If you insist," Sancho groaned and he spurred his donkey forward. "My lady," he called, when he was only a few yards from the riders, "my master, Knight of the Lions, formerly known as Knight of the Long Face, wishes to..."

"Wait," the lady interrupted. "Did you say, Knight of the Long Face?"

Sancho grinned. "Yes, I know it sounds a bit far-fetched but we're out questing, you see. He thinks he's a knight, or perhaps he is a knight, I'm not really sure what he is. And I'm his squire, Sancho..."

"Panza," the lady interrupted again, with a smile.

"That's right," gulped the squire. "Do you know about us then?"

"Of course," she replied. "I have read the book describing you and your gallant master. My husband and I keep a library full of chivalric adventures and *Don Quixote* takes pride of place on our shelves."

"Shall I bring him over then?"

"You may do more than that," said the lady. "Our castle is not far from here. You and your master must stay with us, as our distinguished guests."

"A castle?" Sancho stammered. "A real castle, not the enchanted variety?"

"It is my husband the duke's castle," explained the duchess.

"Cripes," muttered Sancho and the duchess almost giggled. The truth was that she and her husband thought the book, Don Quixote, was the finest comedy ever written. They were great practical jokers, and the duchess reasoned that they'd have some fun with the kooky knight and his dim-witted sidekick. She sent one of her attendants ahead, to warn the duke, then turned her horse and signalled for the squire and knight to follow.

A few minutes later, the party crossed a drawbridge and found themselves in the courtyard of a vast castle, surrounded by maids and pages in red and gold uniforms. Two trumpeters sounded the knight's arrival and a group of handmaidens circled Rocinante, fanning jars of petals and perfumes to

sweeten the air. Above it all, a handsome, middle-aged man waved from a balcony. "Welcome, Don Quixote," cried the duke. "Welcome, to the bravest knight in all of Spain."

The duchess ordered the castle's cooks to prepare a banquet and that night Sancho ate the finest meal of his life. While Don Quixote chatted with his hosts, the squire gorged himself on roast goose, larks tongues pickled in aspic, venison steaks, lambs' kidneys and a whole suckling pig with an apple wedged in its mouth. Sancho had never been happier.

The duke and duchess wore their finest ceremonial costumes and played along with Don Quixote's knightly ravings. They listened attentively to his depiction of the adventure of the lions, the enchanted boat and the joust in the forest. But their greatest interest was in hearing news of Dulcinea. Each time she was mentioned in the novel they'd read, both of them had almost split their sides with hysterics. The idea of a peasant girl being elevated to such chivalric status never ceased to amuse them.

"Would it be rude of me," asked the duke, trying to keep a straight face, "to inquire after your esteemed lady, good knight? Did you send the Knight of the Forest to pay his respects to her, following your victory?"

"I did not," replied Don Quixote, sadly. "My beautiful lady has been transformed into a vulgar, donkey-riding trollop by a mean enchanter."

"How unfortunate," gasped the duchess, barely

able to suppress her giggles.

"My present quest is to find a way to rescue her," the knight continued. "I must break the enchanter's spell and restore my lady to her pristine state."

"I wish you luck in your mission," replied the duchess, glancing mischievously at her husband. "In the meantime, we will try to find a few diversions to take your mind off your lady's plight. Tomorrow, we plan to go hunting for tusked pigs. Will you join us?"

"Alas, kind Duchess," replied the knight, "there is nothing that could take my mind off my Dulcinea. The worth of a man is measured by his loyalty to the things he loves. But I would still be delighted to join your hunting party."

"Me too," cried Sancho, almost hidden behind his enormous plate of food.

The duke's estates stretched for hundreds of miles and included mountains, meadows and dense forests rich with game. Don Quixote and Sancho joined a procession of servants, riders and beaters who left the castle at dawn and wound their way into the heart of a thick forest. By mid-morning they came to a break in the trees, where the duke and duchess awaited their guests.

"Our men will drive the prey towards us," said the duke, taking a lance and shield from one of his servants. "Be on your guard."

"What's all the fuss about?" joked Sancho. "Are you so scared of a few little porkers?"

"We're hunting boar," said the duke. "Wild boar,

huge, tusky brutes that can tear you limb from limb."

"I see," said Sancho, turning white. "In that case, do you mind if I wait for you up a tree?"

"Squire," roared Don Quixote. "Your cowardice shames me. Face the wild boar like a man."

"I've seen enough wild animals to last me a lifetime," cried Sancho. "And I like my limbs just where they are, thank you."

The next instant, there was a crash in the forest and the distant sound of a bugle.

"They've found one," cried the duke. "Beware those gouging tusks."

"Gangway," screamed Sancho, rushing for an oak tree. But Don Quixote grabbed his squire by the britches and lifted him onto Rocinante's rump.

"Don't move a muscle," ordered the knight. "You're safe behind my sword arm."

The trees at the edge of the woods shook and creaked. Sancho heard a bellow and a snort, then the thunder of hooves pounding the forest floor.

"Don't let it get me," he squealed.

"Keep still, you wriggler," growled Don Quixote.

The bushes at the edge of the clearing flew apart and a black stallion appeared before them. It pranced and kicked until Sancho felt dizzy just watching, then he noticed the figure on its back and his blood ran cold. It was a man, all covered in twigs, ivy and leaves. He wore a green mask and had little green horns on the top of his head. In his right hand he carried a green trident.

"I am a forest sprite," the figure shouted, but his

horse was making so much noise they could hardly hear him. "The demons of the forest have sent me with a message for the knight errant, Don Quixote de La Mancha."

"I am Don Quixote," replied the knight. "Calm your horse so I can hear your message."

"I'm trying," said the sprite, struggling with the reins. "But he's a bit frisky."

"Do demons often have trouble with horses?" asked Sancho, hiding behind his master.

"We usually fly everywhere," answered the sprite in a panic. "But I couldn't find my wings today so I had to come on this unruly nag."

"Get on with it," cried the duke, in the same voice he used to reprimand his butler. For in truth, it was the butler there before them, dressed as the sprite of the forest.

"The demons told me," began the sprite, "that they have entranced your lady, Dulcinea, and turned her into an uncouth milk maid."

"That is true," replied Don Quixote, wiping a tear from his eye.

"To free your lady from their spell," the sprite continued, "your squire must agree to lash himself a few times."

"How many times?" screamed Sancho.

"Three thousand, three hundred should do it," replied the sprite.

"What did he say?" gasped Sancho in disbelief.

"But that's not all," warned the sprite. "You must first ride the horse that flies through the air and zooms over mountains. It waits for you at the duke's castle. If you are both brave enough to mount the horse, and Sancho performs the lashes, Dulcinea will be set free."

The sprite tugged on his reins and the stallion bounded into the trees. He left nothing behind but a few leaves fluttering in the air.

"A miracle," sobbed the duchess. "We must return to the keep at once."

"Fetch me a whip," cried Don Quixote. "Sancho can begin his lashing while we ride. Sancho? Come back here, Sancho..."

Back at the castle, there were scenes of pandemonium. The servants were screaming and running around with torches, ringing bells and shouting alarm from the turret-tops. A giant, wooden horse was standing in the middle of the courtyard and the head steward told the duke it had simply dropped out of the air. Don Quixote and Sancho rode in last, arguing – as they had been for the last hour – about the lashes Sancho must suffer to save Dulcinea.

"I tell you again, I refuse to do it," the squire sobbed. "It's not in my contract to lash myself to bits."

"Squires don't have contracts," roared the knight. "I'll tie you to a tree and lash you myself you ungrateful scoundrel."

"Ah, but you can't," said Sancho, shaking his finger in Don Quixote's face. "The lashes don't count unless I do the lashing."

"Then for the sake of my lady, I beg of you, Sancho..."

"Three might be possible," said the squire. "I could do that for you, at a push. But three thousand three hundred is out of the question. I can't even count past fifty."

"You must stop your squabbling," whispered the duchess, leading them into the courtyard. She was enjoying every second of the practical joke she had planned with her husband, and wanted to see the reaction of the knight and squire to the next phase of their scheme. "The flying horse has landed."

Don Quixote stared up at the mighty, wooden statue, towering above him. "What a creature," he gasped in amazement. "It must be twenty feet tall."

Sancho's knees were knocking together with fear. "How are we supposed to climb up to its saddle?" he whimpered.

"There is a rope ladder on the other side," replied the steward.

"Did you see it coming?" asked Sancho. "Did it fly very quickly?"

"Very," said the steward solemnly. "It landed in the blink of an eye."

"Well, this is a fine kettle of fish," sobbed Sancho, turning back to his donkey. "Here I was, at last enjoying the life of a squire my master's been promising me all along. I was eating rich food and sleeping in a feather bed and thinking all the hardship had been worth it. And now look at me. I'm supposed to whip the skin off my backside and fly around on a giant horse."

The duke and duchess overheard the squire's lament and couldn't control their chuckling. When they saw Don Quixote haul himself up the rope ladder, they were almost hooting with laughter and had to hide their faces.

"Come on squire," called the knight. "Stop wasting time talking to your donkey."

"Goodbye, old friend," Sancho whispered into one of the animal's ears. "You probably won't be seeing me again." He shrugged his shoulders and stepped over to the magic steed.

When the squire scrambled onto the smooth wooden back of the giant horse, his whole body was shaking with nerves. There was nothing to hold onto, to help him keep his balance, so he grabbed Don Quixote's trouser belt with both hands.

"Unhand me, you poltroon," barked his master.

"But I'll topple off," squealed Sancho.

"If it wasn't for the fact I have to keep you alive long enough to perform those three thousand lashes, I'd throw you off myself."

"That's not very friendly," said Sancho, looking rather hurt.

"I thought you were my loyal servant," cried Don Quixote. "You should understand my feelings for Dulcinea. How can you hesitate to lash yourself a few times, when you know it would set her free from that awful spell?"

"A few times?" the squire whined. "It's three thousand and three hundred times. There'll be nothing left of me but a scrap of hide."

There was a sudden jolt below them and Sancho gripped the belt even tighter.

"The horse moved," screamed the squire.

"I know it did, you idiot. It's getting ready to take off. Relax, and try to keep your balance. Now let me turn around to face the front."

Don Quixote twisted in the squire's clutch and swung his legs around. At the same time, the horse began rumbling and vibrating, as the duke's servants, hidden inside its wooden frame, began jacking it off the ground.

"There's a carving in the wood here," cried the knight. "It says we have to blindfold ourselves. Anyone who rides the magic horse without a blindfold will be struck dead. What on earth are we going to do?"

"I've got a handkerchief," said Sancho.

"Quick, squire, tear it in two. Blindfold yourself with one half and pass me the other. Hurry..."

The duke and duchess were sitting on a balcony, squealing in mirth as they watched the knight and his squire sliding around on top of the horse. When the riders had fixed Sancho's smelly handkerchief around their faces, the duke lifted his arm to signal his steward. The steward tapped on the wooden horse and the servants inside lifted the horse three feet into the air and rocked it from side to side.

"We're up in the clouds, Sancho," cried Don

Quixote. "What an experience."

"I'm feeling airsick," moaned Sancho. "And the wind's getting up."

The duke and duchess had thought of everything. Four maids were on another balcony next to the head of the horse, working a pair of bellows.

"Brace yourself, Sancho, we're flying through a shower of rain."

Now the maids were dousing the knight and squire with cups of water.

"My head's spinning," cried Sancho. "I feel woozy."

"The air is thin up here," Don Quixote explained. "We must be up in the far reaches of the heavens, flying close to..."

"Close to what?" asked Sancho.

"I'm getting hot," replied the knight.

The duke's butler was leaning over the balcony holding a candle under Don Quixote's beard. The knight sniffed the air and thrashed his head around. "Gadzooks, it's just as I feared," he yelled. "We're flying too high, brushing the surface of the Sun."

"I don't want to be frazzled like a potato chip," sobbed Sancho. "Can't you get us down again?"

The duke was laughing his velvet socks off, but was also feeling a little guilty for playing the prank on the good knight. He signalled to his steward once again, and the servant lit the horse's tail. There was a pop and fizz as hundreds of fireworks hidden inside the tail started to explode. Sancho wrapped his arms around the knight and howled like a puppy. "Save me master. If you do, I promise I'll suffer the lashing."

"All of them?" asked Don Quixote.

"Every skin-splitting one of them," sobbed the squire.

Don Quixote beat the top of the horse with his fists, thinking he could force it to the ground. But the men inside mistakenly took it as a signal to increase their efforts. They rocked the wooden horse so enthusiastically it tilted to one side, lurched too far and crashed to the ground with an ear-crunching thud. Sancho and the knight were thrown to safety, landing on the soft grass of the castle lawn. In the confusion, the servants inside the horse slipped away and took with them all evidence of their handiwork.

When Don Quixote tore the rag from his eyes, he was staring into the face of the duchess who was leaning over him, looking concerned.

"Welcome back," she said softly. "You've been gone for hours and we were getting worried. Did you enjoy the ride?"

The knight and squire rested in their beds for two days, too saddle-sore to move a step. When they had recovered enough strength they joined their hosts in a whirl of lavish dinners, extravagant parties and gentle strolls in the castle grounds. But after a week had passed, Don Quixote struggled into his metal suit and sent a message to his hosts: he would be leaving them that same morning.

"Have we offended you somehow?" cried the

duchess, rushing into the Don's quarters. "Must you leave so soon?"

"I am a knight errant," replied Don Quixote, seriously. "You know it is my duty to wander the Earth, seeking out new adventures and challenges. I am a wrong-righter and good-deeder by nature, madam."

"But what about Sancho's lashing?" asked the duchess, who was anxious not to miss out on the spectacle.

"Squire Panza will carry out his lashing on the hoof, so to speak. He has given me his word on the matter."

"But we were so enjoying your visit," she cried in genuine distress.

"Life at court is softening my sword arm," Don Quixote replied tenderly. "I can never thank you enough for your hospitality, but you must not stand in the way of a knight and his questing."

"You are right, of course," the duchess agreed. "It would be wrong to keep you from your work. Go in peace, good fellow. You are an extraordinary man and I shall never forget you."

Don Quixote bowed to the duchess, dragged the reluctant Sancho from his slumbers, and made his way to the stables. By noon, the two of them were deep in the forest again, heading in the direction of the sea, and the city of Barcelona.

A Knight's Revenge

In which the highs and lows of knight errantry are discovered

"Good squire," cried Don Quixote, rising in the morning from a bed of tree roots, stones and acorn shells. "There is nothing better in this life, than freedom."

"Is that right," said Sancho with a groan. "Can I have my freedom with a pillow attached?" he added, rubbing his aching neck.

"Although we lived a life of luxury at the castle," Don Quixote continued, "I was always malcontent there."

"You've lost me again," replied Sancho, "but if you mean you'd rather sleep on the forest floor than in a feather bed, I say you're bonkers."

"It is a terrible thing to feel indebted to someone, squire. Here in the forest, we don't owe anyone our gratitude except our maker. We are free men, and although we have few possessions, we have no ties or restrictions weighing upon us."

"And no breakfast weighing on our stomachs either," coughed the squire, "...unless you remembered to stock up the saddlebags before you pulled me out of bed."

"The saddlebags are as light and carefree as my heart," replied the knight, stretching his limbs in the sunshine. "Isn't your heart light, Sancho?"

"Oh it is," replied the squire, with a sudden grin. "Except for the two hundred gold escudos the duke's butler slipped me, pressing down on it. He said it's for emergencies and there's no need to worry about paying it back."

"We don't need charity, squire," said the knight.

"Perhaps you don't, but I haven't seen a centavo of my wages yet. And the duke's loaded, so he can spare it. Think of it as a gift."

"Very well," replied the knight. "You may have it as a payment for your lashing. Talking of which..."

"Now don't rush me," cried Sancho, jumping to his feet with surprising agility. "I've done five of them already."

"Five isn't enough," boomed the knight. "You've thousands to get through before my lady is returned to her rightful perfection. And anyway, I haven't seen you do any yet. You told me those five were done in your bedroom at the castle."

"That's right," cried Sancho.

"What proof do I have that you're being truthful?" asked the knight.

"My back's red and raw as though I'd been mauled by a pack of hedgehogs," the squire protested. "There's your proof."

"I'm not satisfied with that. I want to see you do some whipping right this moment."

"We Panzas are very modest," explained the

squire. "I prefer to perform my lashing in private."

"I don't care where you perform it," shouted Don Quixote, "as long it's performed. Conceal yourself if you wish, but I want to hear each lash and know that you're not shirking."

"Very well," snapped Sancho. "I'll get started."

He snatched up the whip that Don Quixote had fixed to the back of his saddle – as a constant reminder of the outstanding lashes – and stomped off between the trees. The squire stopped on the other side of a wide oak, unbuttoned his shirt and tested the whip. He flicked it over his shoulder and cracked it against the tree trunk.

"Ow," he yelped. "That one almost drew blood."

"Splendid," replied the knight. "Keep it up, squire."

Sancho lashed away for ten minutes but all the screaming he was pretending to do made him lose count of the strokes.

"How many is that?" he called to Don Quixote.

"Forty-seven."

"It can't be," squealed Sancho. "My arm's about to drop off it's so tired."

"Continue," barked the knight.

Sancho turned to lash another tree when he noticed something brush the top of his head. He raised a hand and touched a pair of feet. "I'm still dreaming," he whispered to himself, and stepped over to a different tree. But another foot kicked his head and the squire screamed and ran straight back to the camp.

"What are you doing?" asked the knight. "Back to your lashing."

"The trees have got legs," cried Sancho.

"Don't be ridiculous," Don Quixote barked. 'Trees don't go walking about do they? They don't take strolls in the park or dash to the shops."

"Look for yourself," the squire whimpered.

Don Quixote stepped past the oak tree and peered into the branches above him. "Bandits," he whispered.

"Where?" cried Sancho, tiptoeing behind him.

"Up there, squire," said the knight, bobbing a thumb upwards.

"What are they doing up there?" asked Sancho.

"They're dead, squire," said Don Quixote, flatly. "The authorities sometimes hang bandits in the woods, as a warning to other criminals."

"Well, that's a relief," panted Sancho.

"Is it?" answered Don Quixote. "It means we're in the middle of bandit country. The place must be swarming with them."

"Dead ones, you mean?" asked Sancho.

"No, squire, the living, breathing variety."

"Absurd," laughed Sancho. "No bandit would dare to lurk in a copse full of corpses. These feet would scare them off."

Sancho leaned down and picked up a stick. He struck a pair of feet hanging from one of the trees.

"Ow," said a rough voice from up in the leaves.

Sancho dropped the stick. He started running towards his donkey but before he'd gone three paces he was surrounded by a gang of fierce-looking bandits. Don Quixote tried to push his way back to the camp for his weapons but the bandits threw him to the ground.

"Let's chop off their heads," hissed one of the gang.

"I'd like to," said another. "But the chief will be here in a minute. He'll want to see this for himself."

Ten, nervous minutes later, the brigand chief arrived on a white stallion. He was a good-looking villain, tanned and burly. The tools of his trade were proudly displayed on his body. A great sword was strapped across his back and he wore four pistols on a belt around his waist. One of his men took his horse's reins and the chief dropped to the ground

and approached the prisoners.

"A knight in the forest," he guffawed, when he saw Don Quixote standing there in his shabby metal suit. "But where is your lance?"

"If I had had my lance," replied Don Quixote coolly, "every one of your swarthy colleagues would be lying dead at my feet."

The chief walked across to the camp and examined the knight's weapons. "If I didn't know better," he began, "I'd say you were the spitting image of that Don Quixote loony."

"I am not a loony," replied the knight firmly.

"But he's only a literary invention, a character in a book," gasped the bandit. "He doesn't exist."

"Pass me my sword and you'll see if I exist," roared

Don Quixote.

"Then I am at your service," said the chief, bowing almost to the ground. "Release them," he ordered his men, "and make camp."

Don Quixote and Sancho watched in amazement as the bandits led a line of donkeys through the trees, each one loaded with heavy packs, chairs, even the dissembled sections of a table. In a few minutes the bandit chief was lounging on a divan, digging in to a silver platter of grapes, cheeses and chorizo sausage.

"First," he politely requested, "you will tell me of your recent adventures. I want to be able to steal the march on my friends with all the news about *Don Quixote PART TWO*. Next, I will provide you with an escort to the boundaries of Barcelona and my friends there can ride with you to the town hall. You will be the toast of the city, Don Quixote. Everyone has read your adventures. People will line the streets to welcome you, and cheer your name to the sky."

Sancho and his master had never seen the sea before. When their bandit guides led them onto a hilltop overlooking the Mediterranean, the knight and squire sat in silence, gazing across the blue wastes of water.

"What are those?" the squire asked, pointing at what he thought were blocks of wood, bobbing on the surface.

"Galleons," whispered the knight. "I have seen pictures of them in books. They carry hundreds of men, across thousands of miles of open water and some have forty cannons lined below their decks."

As he said this one of the ships let off a broadside. Sancho saw a cloud of white smoke rush out and around the side of the ship. Seconds later, he heard a boom in the air and he ducked his head instinctively. "Are they firing at us?" he cried.

"Today is a fiesta," explained one of the bandits. "The king's ships are out on exercises, showing off their guns."

Don Quixote stared along the beach, all the way around the bay to the glinting rooftops of Barcelona. A group of riders in bright clothes suddenly burst out of the city gates and galloped towards them.

"Those are the chief's friends," said the bandit. "They'll look after you from here."

The bandits melted back into the trees and the knight and his squire waited apprehensively for their next escort. When the men arrived, they shook hands with Don Quixote and put a garland of red roses around his neck.

"The streets are teeming with your fans," shouted one of them. "You'll ride into our town in glory."

Everything was just as the bandit chief had predicted. News of the celebrity knight and squire coming to Barcelona had spread from bar to bar, to schools, offices and private houses. The citizens thronged the cobbled lands, trying to catch a glimpse of the crazy but noble knight and his mischievous squire. They threw flowers and sweets, cheered the names of their heroes and argued over which was the most impressive of their fantastic adventures.

The leader of the escort offered Don Quixote the free use of his villa in the heart of the town. That night, the bemused friends dined on a terrace overlooking the city and the sea, with legions of their supporters praising them from the streets below.

For two weeks they lived like kings. The mayor of Barcelona gave them the keys to the city, they were visited by admirals, generals and high-ranking public officials, and wherever they wandered in the town they were greeted like long-lost sons.

"This is better than that island you promised me," Sancho said to his master one day, as he helped himself to a huge bowl of paella.

"It is good to have one's achievements celebrated," agreed the knight. "But remember, friend, too much easy living is not to my liking. It softens the spirit."

"I'll take a lifetime of it," laughed Sancho. "Think of the good we could do, touring from one city to the next, greeting the citizens and instructing them on the benefits of duty and the chivalric way of life."

"You speak of chivalry and duty, squire," said Don Quixote. "How have your lashes been going lately?"

"I've been too busy for any of that," Sancho replied, coughing on a spoonful of rice.

"I suspected as much," said the knight. "You see how all this luxury has swerved you from the noble path? The sooner we get back to questing the better it will be for you."

While he remained in the city, it was Don Quixote's habit to rise at dawn and take Rocinante for a trot along the beach. He was out on one of these morning jaunts when he saw a figure approaching him on the sands. It was a man riding alone, and his clothes glinted in the sun. He was

wearing a full suit of arms and his visor was lowered.

Sensing an adventure, the old hidalgo urged Rocinante into a canter. When he got nearer to the stranger he could see the emblem on his shield was a white, crescent moon.

"Halt, Knight of the Lions," called the Knight of the White Moon. "I have a challenge for you."

"Don Quixote is always ready for a challenge," answered the hidalgo, bravely.

"Then we will joust," said the stranger, raising a shiny new lance.

"Excellent," cried Don Quixote. "I need to thrash rascally young knights like yourself to keep myself in trim. Name your terms."

"If you win, my lance and this fine horse are yours as the spoils of war. Should I be the victor, you must retire, with immediate effect."

"Retire?" cried Don Quixote. "That is impossible."

"We young knights," explained the Knight of the White Moon, "are growing tired of an old rooster like yourself getting all the public's attention in Spain. We want you to return to your village for a year and live a peaceful life, so we can have a fair chance at glory."

"I respect your ambition, but I'm in my prime," roared Don Quixote. "Retirement would be the same as death."

"So, are you scared to do battle, old man?"

"You insolent pup," snapped the hidalgo. "I accept your terms."

Both knights turned away from each other and checked their weapons. The Knight of the White Moon kicked his horse into a gallop and bore down on Don Quixote. He held his lance with such flair and precision, the elderly knight didn't stand a chance against him. He was lifted out of his saddle and dumped in the breakers. In a flash, the Knight of the White Moon had dismounted and was pressing his bronze sword into Don Quixote's windpipe.

"Concede?" he cried. "You are vanquished, so concede."

"But it means the end of my life," sobbed Don Quixote. "Without chivalry, I am nothing."

"You gave your word," the victor snarled.

"I will retire," coughed Don Quixote, "for a year, as promised." The defeated hidalgo's tears mixed with the salt water of the waves that lapped around his iron suit. "This is the darkest day of all my adventures," he added with a moan.

But the Knight of the White Moon showed no pity. He remounted his stallion and left the broken hidalgo sobbing in the surf.

The Done Don

In which Don Quixote and Sancho make the final sally

Don Quixote hobbled back to town, never guessing that his opponent on the beach was Carrasco, the student from his village. In the months since his defeat, posing as the Knight of the Forest, the priest's assistant had been studying the arts of horsecraft and jousting. He was determined both to have his revenge on Don Quixote for the bruises he had suffered, and to return the loopy hidalgo to his anxious friends in the village.

Once outside the city limits, Carrasco dumped his metal suit and bought some provisions for the road ahead. Don Quixote however, was busy rousing Sancho and describing the disaster on the beach.

"You can't quit now," sobbed the squire. "Old dogs don't learn new tricks."

"I gave my word," replied the knight. "Strip this suit of arms from me, Sancho. I no longer need it."

"Oh master," the squire pleaded with him. "What will we do instead of questing now? I was almost getting to like it."

"Pack our bags," said Don Quixote, still tearful.

"There is a three day ride ahead of us, and I wish to leave at once."

On a lonely hill above the city, Don Quixote halted Rocinante and studied the glittering bay stretching along the rim of the Mediterranean. "Scholars will remember this place," he sighed, "as the last stand of the brave Knight of the Lions. Poets will compose lines about my tumble into the waves. Pilgrims will come to visit, and perhaps even a modest shrine will be built as tribute to my glorious deeds, in the days before I was vanquished."

"You're a bit gloomy aren't you?" cried Sancho at his side. "I've been thinking about the promise you made. It was to retire for a year wasn't it? Well, what's one year to old veterans like us?"

"I don't follow you, squire."

"When the year's over you can take up your lance again."

"If I am fit and well at the year's end," replied Don Quixote, "of course I will go questing again. But already I feel a fever creeping into my bones, old friend. When a knight is toppled in a joust, it is not just his pride that is broken. I will have to accept that my best days are behind me."

"Don't be so downhearted, sir," Sancho appealed.

"From now on you must not call me sir. I have been stripped of my title and am a simple commoner now."

Before Sancho could utter another word, Don Quixote kicked Rocinante into a trot and took off along the path.

That night they made camp by a stream. Sancho had been trying to lift Don Quixote's spirits throughout the day, but to no avail. The ex-knight was simply inconsolable.

"Isn't there anything I can do to cheer you up?" the squire asked him. "I'd go without food if it would make you happy."

"If I knew that my lady was safe," said Don Quixote, "I might be able to smile again."

Sancho sighed. "Will I never escape those lashes? I could do a thousand or two, I suppose."

"I would be grateful, squire."

So Sancho wandered off into some nearby woods, found a suitable tree and lashed it for an hour. With each stroke he let out a blood-chilling howl and Don Quixote called out the number of lashes still remaining. When Sancho had reached five hundred, the hidalgo jumped up from his seat by the fire. "Oh squire," he cried in his concern, "your poor back must be crisscrossed with terrible cuts and bruises from all this whipping. Don't you need a rest?"

"I can't afford to rest," sobbed Sancho, hidden behind the tree. "My pain means nothing compared to restoring the rightful beauty of your lady."

"Spoken like a true knight," Don Quixote whispered to himself.

"There is one thing you could do to help though," said the squire.

"Name it, you brave man," replied the hidalgo.

"Just fix me a few sandwiches," answered the squire. "Leave them on the other side of the tree so

I can reach around for them, between lashes."

When Sancho had lashed all the bark off the tree, Don Quixote informed him he'd suffered a thousand lashes and must stop before he killed himself. The squire limped back to his blankets by the fire and sipped wine to restore his strength.

"I am proud of you," Don Quixote told him warmly. "If you can manage a thousand a night, Dulcinea will be free by the time we reach our village."

"It is a small price to pay," the squire wheezed, "to see my master smiling."

The two friends rode hard each day, passing through the duke's forests, along the banks of the River Ebro and steadily retracing their steps across the mountains and down into the plains of La Mancha. After they made camp, Sancho would find his whipping post and rack up another thousand lashes. On the morning of the fourth day, he got up at dawn and finished the last two hundred and forty-eight lashes. Don Quixote shook his squire's hand and promised to double his salary if they ever went questing again.

"So you think we might?" cried Sancho in his excitement.

"I hope so, squire. Do you see those shepherds over there?" The hidalgo pointed to some men out on the plain, only a few miles from their village.

"That might be Pepe," replied Sancho, "and Alvarez his son. They're old friends of mine."

"Are they poets as well as shepherds?" Don Quixote asked.

"They like a song and a good story," answered the squire, "if that's the same thing?"

"I suppose it is," said Don Quixote, his eyes sparkling.

"But what are you getting at?" asked Sancho, rubbing his head.

"Now that my lady is free, and I am forbidden to go out questing, I have decided to become a shepherd."

"But you're a man of arms," laughed the squire. "You carry a lance, not a crook."

"It will only be for a year," replied Don Quixote. "Then I will return to my chivalric calling. But do you remember, in the Moreno Mountains I once told you that knights are poetic creatures at heart?"

"I remember."

"Well, so are shepherds. They wander the country, looking after the weak – in their case, their flock – and spend most of each day lost in their thoughts. If I am suspended from being a knight for a year, then the life of a shepherd will suit me fine."

"It's more peaceful than questing," agreed Sancho, nodding his head.

"And peace is just what I need," replied Don Quixote, with a smile. "I will compose poetry for my lady, and tell stories around the campfire about all the glorious adventures we had. Now let's break camp and ride into our village. We should be there in time for breakfast."

But the careful plans of men come and go like clouds across a summer sky. When Don Quixote rode into the courtyard of his hacienda, the housekeeper was out hanging washing. She dropped her basket in the dust and ran over to hug him. "Master, you're back in one piece," she cried.

"I am weak," whispered Don Quixote. "Sancho, help me to my room."

Back in his old four-poster bed, the hidalgo slipped into a sleep that lasted for six days. The fever that had been with him since his fall on the beach intensified. He raved and groaned as though plagued by nightmares, while his friends waited patiently by his bedside. After a week, Don Quixote opened his eyes and saw the priest and barber sitting at the foot of the bed.

"I am back," the hidalgo muttered.

"Don Quixote," they shouted, rushing over to him.

"My name is Alonso Quixano," said the man in the bed. "I have been mad, but now my mind is restored."

"Is it true?" gasped the priest. "Are all thoughts of chivalry and dragons and damsels really gone from your head?"

"They are all gone," the hidalgo replied softly, "and I am sane enough to know that I am dying. You must hear my confession at once."

The news that the hidalgo was on his deathbed raced around the village. Sancho came running from where he had been working in the fields. When the priest had finished his work, the squire was shown in and he knelt by the side of his former master.

"Perhaps you were a little mad," Sancho began, tears streaming over his cheeks. "But there is nothing more mad than to die of grief. And I know that it is grief that is killing you. If you were still a knight, you would not die."

"Your friend," replied the hidalgo, "the man who was a knight... he is no longer here. You must forget him."

"I cannot," sobbed the squire.

"You will receive the wages he owed you," the hidalgo promised. "Use the money to build a good life for yourself."

Sancho wanted to persuade his old friend not to give up the ghost, but the hidalgo was overcome by his fever. His squire kept a vigil over him, until he slipped out of the living world, just three days later.

This was the end of the brave knight, Don Quixote de la Mancha, Knight of the Lions, formerly known as Knight of the Long Face. In his madness, he accomplished feats that ordinary men can only dream of. His story has been told for four hundred years, and his spirit shines on, across the sun-scorched plains of southern Spain. Rest in Peace, noble Don Quixote. May the questing be good and the adventures to your liking...

About Miguel de Cervantes

It might be no surprise that the creator of a character as fantastic as Don Quixote had an eventful and extraordinary life. Miguel de Cervantes was born near Madrid, Spain, in 1547, only a few years before Shakespeare. His father, a barber and part-time surgeon, had financial troubles and, like so many writers in history, Cervantes always struggled with money. Perhaps in an attempt to improve his position, he joined the army in 1570, signing up with a Spanish regiment based in Naples, Italy.

But his days in the military marked the start of a run of bad luck. He was wounded at the Battle of Lepanto in 1571 and lost the use of his left hand. Maimed and growing tired of soldiering, he took a ship across the Mediterranean, only to be attacked by pirates and sold into slavery in North Africa. It took five years for his friends and family to arrange a ransom for his release. Arriving home, he worked as a clerk helping to provision the Spanish Armada and then as a tax collector. But his luck hadn't changed and he was twice thrown into prison, for discrepancies in his accounts. During his second spell behind bars, he started to shape the character of the crazed hidalgo, Don Quixote. He quickly made a plan for the book that would change his life forever.

Cervantes had already published some poetry and plays before he started work on his novel, but with little success. He decided it was vital to capture the interest of his audience from the very first page. This is why the opening chapters of *Don Quixote* are short and fast-moving, and the battle with the windmills – the most famous of the knight's adventures – comes so early on. It was only when Sancho Panza's coarse character began to sparkle next to the knight's stuffiness that Cervantes realized he had created something special. He spent five years creating *Part one* of the adventure, ready for publication in 1605.

The book was a sensation, acclaimed throughout Europe, especially in England, where it was translated in 1612. At last, at the age of 58, Cervantes had broken his spell of bad luck. But it wasn't to last. He foolishly sold the rights to his book and was impoverished again within a few years. To make matters worse, a sequel appeared in 1614, penned by a mystery scribe. Cervantes was so enraged he wrote his own sequel a year later, mocking the author of the copycat book in the first chapter, when Carrasco describes it to the irritated knight and squire.

This time, Cervantes made sure there wouldn't be any further sequels. He killed off his creation, to protect the reputation of his work from further shoddy imitations. Perhaps he knew he was coming to the end of his own life, when he described Don Quixote rejecting his chivalric delusions on his deathbed. Only a few months after *Part two* was published, in 1616, Cervantes died in Madrid. But the deranged knight he had dreamed up in his prison cell remains one of the world's most famous literary characters, almost four centuries later.